A Cougar Among Wolves

Black Hills Wolves Book 45

By
Kali Willows

This book is a work of fiction. Names, characters, places, and incidents are the products of the author's imagination or used fictitiously. Any resemblance to actual events, locales or persons, living or dead, is entirely coincidental.

Copyright © 2016 by Kali Willows
ISBN: 978-1-68361-007-6
Cover art by Fiona Jayde

Published by Decadent Publishing Company, LLC
Look for us online at:
www.decadentpublishing.com

Praise for *A Cougar Among Wolves*

With this tale Willows combines the worst of humanity with the best of characters who have heart ~ Amazon Reviewer

Kali Willows puts her characters through hell in order to get to their HEA. A fast paced, heart wrenching tale of love found ~ Amazon Reviewer

[A Cougar Among Wolves] *has all the elements to make a great read, suspense, drama, action, love, hawt scenes and quite a few surprise discoveries that will answer so many questions for their kind in the future* ~ Amazon Reviewer

2 Sexy young wolves+ 1 Smokin hot redheaded Cougar= EXPLOSIVE chemistry....~ Amazon Reviewer

Whoooo what a book! 2 brothers, 1 girl. Nuff said ~ Amazon Reviewer

~A Note from the Author~

Thank you for choosing A Cougar Among Wolves for your reading pleasure! This story takes a dark turn with danger and the strive for survival, tempered with passion and healing for a heroine who thought there was no hope left after a devastating attack. It shows how cultures in the paranormal world can mix and mingle, and band together for continued existence and recovery in an unrelenting world of greed and brutality. It's steamy but riveting. I hope you enjoy it as much as I did writing it.

Happy Reading,

Kali Willows

Dedication

To Kacey Hammell, Kayleigh Malcolm and JoAnne Kenrick, you are all my partners in crime. Without your feedback, I wouldn't have the divine privilege to continue to grow as an author. Critique partners are a crucial component in bringing our stories to life. Your words inspire, your support and encouragement mean the world to me, thank you for being there.

Thank you to Rebecca Royce, for welcoming me into the Black Hills Wolves world and encouraging me to stick with the story, your guidance and tutelage of the pack was fantastic!

To Bev Kyte, my biggest fan. Your smile, your enthusiasm and your unwavering love for my stories always make me want to write more.

Prologue

G riffith yanked on the broken iron handle of the dingy wooden door and held it open for her. A blast of raunchy guitar riffs and heavy bass reverberated in her delicate ears. Klaya skulked inside to find what she expected from the local watering hole.

The retched gust of sour beer shot up her sensitive nose and brought bile to the back of her throat.

"Really?" She whipped around and glared at her older brother. "We couldn't find someplace less...disgusting?"

"Come on, it's Utah. It's not like you'll find swanky New York nightclubs here. Where's your sense of adventure?" He chuckled and strolled ahead of her toward the grubby bar.

"Adventure? I don't consider bathing in smelly

1

filth an adventure." She followed him as she grimaced.

A few steps in, she tripped on the uneven wooden floor and slammed into Griffith's back. He spun around and steadied her with his hands on her shoulders. "You okay?"

"Peachy," she retorted, eyeing the grimy rolled-copper bar.

Several patrons tittered and she glared at them. Some of the mangled wooden chairs were held together with tattered layers of silver duct tape. Most had spindles missing from the backs. Coasters tucked under the legs of the dozen or so square tables indicated an attempt to stop them from wobbling.

"Charming." With another slow, cautious inhale, something else settled on her palate. She leaned close to her brother's ear. "We aren't the only shifters in here."

"I know," he replied. "I smell a wolf, too, but I don't sense any danger."

She counted sixteen patrons throughout the bar and one tall, gangly man with greasy blond hair and a tattered yellow T-shirt filling a pitcher with beer from a hose behind the counter. From every corner, the wall-mounted speakers pumped heavy metal music, torturing her tender ears.

"I'll buy the first round, your favorite." Griffith plopped down on a wooden stool at the bar and patted the empty seat beside him.

"Fine, but I doubt they'd serve a tequila sunrise here. Shots of booze and beer are all you'll get."

"It's wet, and it's booze. what's the problem?" He snickered.

"You're buying me more than one round." She eased herself onto the uneven-legged barstool, the sticky grime on the surface snagging at the seat of her jeans. "For the record," she hissed, "I hate you."

"Barkeep," Griffith called out over the noise. "A round of tequila shots and beers." He gestured between the two of them. "And one for this guy at the end of the bar."

The solitary drinker hunched over clutching a beer. Dark-haired, with a scowl marring his handsome features, the distinct presence of trouble and bitterness emanated from him. Amid the brash vibrations of the loud music and chatter, her acute hearing honed in on other sounds, including the clanking of beer bottles on table tops and scuffing of shoes across the bar floor. The occasional grunt from the guy at the end suggested he was in a foul mood, and likely, already inebriated.

"Are you sure he needs another?" She spoke close to her brother's ear.

"Looks like he's had a run of bad luck." Griffith accepted the three shot glasses from the bartender and reached for the lime wedges in a bowl on the counter along with a shaker of salt. "Hey, buddy, care for a round?" He held up a glass.

The scowl lightened, and he picked up his beer and limped toward them, favoring his left leg.

"Thanks." The man took the glass and tossed it back, snagged a lime, and sucked on it. "Mighty kind of you."

He turned to leave, but her smartass brother couldn't leave well enough alone. "The name is Griffith, and this is my little sister, Klaya."

The man faced them and curled his lip. "Hi."

Desperate to escape, she shifted to the edge of her barstool. "How ya doin'?"

"I've been better," he slurred.

A powerful scent wafted up her nose. *I smell a wolf.* But she detected no danger from him whatsoever.

After a few more rounds of tequila, the slovenly stranger spilled his guts about being shunned from

4

his town, explaining he was now on the run and his limp was a result of a gunshot by one of his father's cronies. A profound sense of compassion filled Klaya, along with the heated trickle of alcohol down her solar plexus. "I'm so sorry you've had to go through all that, Drew."

"Thanks." He nodded. Now on the barstool between her and Griffith, he confided even more. "The worst is I can't be with my Betty."

"Hey, will you two be okay if I excuse myself for a second?" Griffith arched his brows. "Nature calls."

"Sure." She didn't mind her new company. Knowing his story, she felt terrible for the guy. Klaya downed another shot of tequila and chased it with a beer. "I'm sure things will work out for you."

"Cheers to that." He clinked bottles with her then set his on the counter, and buried his head in his arms.

Klaya chuckled. The guy was going to hurt in the morning.

A massive man with exceptionally dirty, long, black hair and a bulky leather jacket took a seat on the stool on her other side. Based on his bone structure, dark eyes, and tanned complexion, she estimated him to be of Native American descent. His protruding forehead gave off a Cro-Magnon air, complementing his thick, undefined lips.

"Hey, Johnny boy," he bellowed. "Gimme a beer and one for the lady."

The bartender rushed over, popped the beer caps off with shaky hands, and slid them in front of the brute. "O-on the house, Jimmy."

"I thought so." The man leered at Klaya, slid a bottle in front of her, and then growled, "Hey, gorgeous. This is for you."

She reeled back. "Uh...thanks, but I've got my own." She held up her drink. "And I'm done for the night." She inched away, nostrils stinging from his pungent body odor.

"You'll have another." He chugged his beer.

"No, I won't." She gritted her teeth. "But thank you."

The Neanderthal slammed his bottle on the counter. "I bought you a drink. You should be grateful."

"No, you bullied the bartender to get it for free, and you decided to tell me what to do. That's not gonna happen, so disappear." She let out a guttural growl of caution. Another unappealing whiff confirmed he was both human and grotesque. The barbarian loomed over her. "I said—"

"The lady told you to get lost." Her new buddy managed to pull himself out of his drunken stupor and got to his feet. "Now, walk away from my friend here, or I'll rip you from limb to limb," Drew roared, teetering, his fists clenched so tight his knuckles whitened.

The gargantuan crowded over Drew and gave a vicious glower. He was no less than an entire foot taller than him with shoulders double his own width. Klaya glanced down. The tyrant's feet were twice the size of Drew's. *This will not end well.*

"Boys," she grumbled and stood. Inserting herself as a barricade between the pending collision of testosterone, she glared up at her unwanted suitor. "There's no need to cause a scene."

"Then you'll have the drink?"

"No." She crossed her arms and lifted her chin.

Without warning, the man shot his right fist out over Klaya's shoulder. A loud crack behind her was followed by a heavy thud on the floor.

A quick glance revealed her newfound friend out cold. "Are you kidding me?" She fired her left knee into the huge guy's groin, and he dropped like a sack of potatoes, gripping his crotch and wheezing.

"I can't leave you alone for a minute," Griffith chuckled behind her.

Klaya swung around to find her brother lifting an unconscious Drew off the floor and slinging the lad's arm over his shoulder.

"Well, are you gonna stick around for him to retaliate, or are you gonna help me get this guy out of here before he's used as a mop for this filthy floor?"

"Now you take issue with the cleanliness?" she scoffed.

Still on his knees, Jimmy grabbed her wrist as she turned to follow her brother. She tugged out of his grasp, curled her fingers in and gave a hard pummel to his nose. Cro-Magnon man dropped flat on his back.

Chapter One

A thunderous crack rang out. A lightning bolt of horrendous pain splayed from her shoulder along the length of her spine from the impact of the bullet. Klaya dropped onto her stomach but forced herself to claw her way along the bed of dry leaves. A fierce growl escaped her lips. Multiple crunching footsteps echoed throughout the dreary forest, closing in fast.

"It went over there," a hoarse voice called.

Crackles of branches and twigs echoed in her ears as the men traipsed through the trees. Their steps drew closer. She had to hide before they found her.

Ahead, she spotted a massive tree with overgrown roots protruding from the ground. Light showed through the base of the tree, promising a hollow safe haven if she could make it there before they located her. Klaya scampered despite the searing pain of the gunshot wound. Shivering, she fought the overriding fatigue and blood loss and clawed under the roots to gain asylum.

She squeezed through the narrow hole and curled inside. Unable to maintain her form any longer, Klaya hitched her breath, desperate not to cry out during the change. Her claws retracted as did her tail. Her fur disappeared, and, in its place, her skin and hair materialized.

The voices drew nearer. "It's close, but I'm getting interference with the signal. Must be the trees. Got a blood trail," another man called out. "Bring in the hounds. It's around here somewhere."

Klaya stared through the hole. With no one in sight yet, she stuck her shaking hand out and dragged an armful of leaves toward her to shield her location. At the top of the pile, a tiny ray of light peered in and provided a line of sight she could spy through. She panted, her mouth grew dry, and she trembled from head to toe. An icy sting encased her upper back and spread through her limbs. The distant sound of barking rang in her ears. Not twenty yards from where she cowered, four men gathered with rifles, and even more heavy footsteps crunched toward her, rubber soles scuffing against exposed tree roots.

"Look, right there, two of them." The man with dark hair and a beard took a single step back and snarled. "Son of a bitch, this is turning out to be a hell of a day, boys." He lifted his rifle.

Horror pumped through her as he aimed the gun in her direction. Klaya's parched lips cracked and her throat stung from dryness. Leaves rustled outside her wooden shelter. A sudden bark beside her sounded, followed by vicious growls and bloodcurdling screams of terror. A blurred commotion of fur, crimson splatter, and ear-piercing gunshots ensued.

She sank into the cold dirt and faded into blackness.

Seth let out a deep growl and licked his curled lip. The fur on his neck spiked as he stood next to the tree, fearless in the face of the humans with their pitiful weapons. Behind the men, his brother Rogue crept up. The hounds on chains went crazy. They barked and tried to yank away from their masters. Seth crouched in wait for the ambush. Rogue vaulted onto the shoulders of the one pointing the rifle and knocked him to the ground. In a rage-filled frenzy, he ripped the jugular open and moved onto the next one who lifted his gun to aim.

Snarling, Seth tackled the last two assassins. Within seconds of ferocious bites and tearing of flesh, the four men lay in a bloody pile upon the ground. The hounds barked and advanced. Seth growled and towered over them. The inferior canines yelped and hightailed it out of the forest, leaving the slain humans behind.

His brother trotted to his side, licking the blood off his own lips, and growled. Searching for signs of any more threats in the area, Seth lifted his head and sniffed the air. The powerful and alluring scent of cougar hidden in the confines of the tree dulled most other smells, but amid the odor of death, he sensed no further need for protection. Certain it was clear, he tucked his head down and allowed the transformation to begin. He dug his nails into the earth and braced his shoulders as the sting of shifting took over from his ears to his paws. Rogue followed and turned as well. Once the shift was complete, he got up from his hands and knees. The adrenaline still coursed through his veins; his body quaked with the residual power of the shift.

A little slower to recover, Rogue rested on his knees and inhaled a deep breath. He raked his fingers through his mangy hair.

The scent of copper wrapped around him. "I can smell the blood. She's hurt bad." Seth scrambled to the base of the tree.

His brother clambered to his side, and they worked fast to dig a wider opening at the base of the tree.

"Jesus." Seth reeled back, his breath caught in his throat. "She's covered in blood...."

"Never mind. She's hurt." Rogue cleared out the hole under the tree.

The brothers reached in and took hold of her limp arms. A lightning bolt of energy stabbed through Seth's hands.

"What the hell?" He recoiled. "Did you see that?"

"I didn't just see it. I felt it." Rogue shook his hand. "What happened?"

"I don't know, but it was weird. Are you okay?"

"Yeah, it stung a little, but now it's a warm buzz crawling up my arm."

"Me, too." Seth inspected his hands. Static shock tickled the pads of his fingers and his palms. "Try again? We have to get her out of there."

Rogue nodded.

This time, they reached with caution and made contact with her skin. Nothing happened. "Okay.". They carefully dragged the woman out.

"She looks like hell." Rogue placed his palm on

her forehead. "Her body temp is high."

"They shot her close to the spine. It looks pretty bad."

"Man, she's gorgeous." Rogue rested on his knees and stared at her face.

"Focus, buddy. We have to get her to Los Lobos." Seth grazed his fingers over the puncture wound as blood seeped out.

"Are you crazy? We can't show up with an outsider. Ryker would kick our asses. So would Drew!"

"Bastian's a doctor. We'll go to him."

Rogue's eyes filled with worry. "He's governed by pack law, too. Anything we do has to go through Ryker or Drew. You know this, and we're wasting time discussing it."

"The park ranger station is about fifteen minutes on foot. I will carry her, but you shift and run ahead to give Wyatt the heads-up, and call Ryker and Bastian, ask them to meet us there. I'll bring her to the ranger station."

"Either way, if the enforcer doesn't already know she's here, he will soon, and he'll want to know about those guys." Rogue gestured to the massacre.

"They had more friends with them. I'm guessing

they'll return for their buddies, or for payback," Seth concurred. "At least, there, Ryker won't tear us a new one for bringing her into town and the hunters that were after her."

"I can't let her see me like this." Seth motioned to his naked body. "She might wake up."

"We weren't planning on mingling. We didn't bring any clothes." His brother fired him a curt glare.

"She's bleeding to death. We don't have much time. Forget the clothes," he snarled.

"Good point, but we need to bandage her wound." Desperate to slow the bleeding, Seth stripped a coat and T-shirt off one of the dead guys. The brothers tore the cotton shirt into strips and did their best. They tied the remainder of the black cloth to hold the makeshift bandages in place. As Seth draped a jacket over the naked woman, a glimmer caught his eye. He spotted a silver collar around her neck, holding a metal charm a quarter size of his palm. He held it and studied it. Celtic knotwork was embossed in the metal, and words he couldn't read. Were they Gaelic? Time continued slipping away. He rested the charm against her chest then scooped up her frail body.

"Go now. I'll be close behind." He nodded to

7

Rogue.

Rogue completed the shift in seconds, faster than usual, and then bolted off toward the south.

Adrenaline coursed through Seth's veins, he glanced down at the mysterious redhead. "I hope you make it." He raced after his brother.

Chapter Two

The muscles in his thighs strained as Seth climbed the steps to the ranger station. The warm buzz from his first contact with the mysterious woman had spread from his arms to his chest and down his sternum. A deep-seated ache took hold in the race to get her to safety.

The screen door flew open, and Bastian rushed out to meet him. "I came as soon as I got the call. Is she breathing?" He glanced over her quickly.

"Yeah," Seth huffed.

"Wyatt isn't here. He's out on park business. The table is set up in the office over there," he directed.

The last of the strength in Seth's arms and legs waned as he carried her to the door behind the front desk and placed her on the portable steel table covered in white linen. Upon releasing her, the warm tingles subsided and were soon replaced by the ache of stiff muscles from the rush through the forest to get her to safety.

The pack doctor lifted her lids and shone a small light in each eye then held her wrist and studied his watch. "Her stats aren't the greatest, but she's steady for now. I need to see her wound."

Rogue helped Seth position her on her side to give access to her gunshot.

Scissors in hand, Bastian snipped off the makeshift bandages. He grabbed gauze and a bottle of antiseptic to clean the injuries.

"Okay, boys, fill me in." Doc worked away.

"Does Ryker know yet?"

"He does," a stern voice answered from the doorway.

"Ryker." Rogue sighed. "You're fast."

A dull ache filled Seth's chest as he stared at the unconscious redhead. "We were on a run around the perimeter of the territory and caught this incredible scent." He sucked in another breath and savored the luscious aroma. "It was so...."

"Provocative," Rogue finished for him.

"We smelled humans nearby and heard yelling and gunshots." Seth recounted the events.

"Is she human?" Bastian cocked his head and

inspected the patient with arched brows.

"No," Rogue answered, tension in the single syllable. "She's a cougar. Her scent was so powerful."

"Continue," Ryker prompted.

"A pack of hunters were tracking her, like a deer. They shot her from behind, the cowards," he snarled. "She burrowed into a hole under a huge oak tree to hide."

"Any survivors? Witnesses?" The enforcer maintained his cold stare.

"No witnesses, but...." Rogue confessed.

"But?"

"Their buddies took off. We could smell them, but they weren't in our sights. Three more." Unease coursing through his veins, Seth approached Ryker. The enforcer wouldn't have hesitated about pursuing the other hunters and the threat would have been eliminated right then and there. The choices he and his brother made put the rest of the pack at risk and Ryker and Drew would see they had failed them. The prospect of disappointing them tied his stomach in knots.

"What direction?" His dark eyes narrowed.

"They headed east. We didn't have time to hunt them down. She would have bled to death." Seth gritted his teeth, his guilty conscience warring with his need to defend his actions.

Thankfully, Rogue gripped his arm, silencing him. "What do you want us to do about it?"

Pausing, Ryker stared at the woman. "Nothing." Then, he switched his attention to Bastian. "Is she gonna make it?"

"I think so." Bastian dug into her flesh with long metal prongs. "I have to get her over to my office and test her blood type. I hope I have the right kind. I've got the bullet." He drew the small, cylindrical metal slug out and dropped it into the pan on the table with a clink. He scanned her bloodied body, lifted her left arm, and inspected another wound. Blood oozed along her forearm, and Bastian wiped it down, but it kept bleeding. "This isn't a gunshot, but there's something in there." He dug the surgical tool into her forearm at the point of entry and gripped then pulled it out. He held a thin square up in the air.

The pack doctor steeled his back and faced Ryker. "We have a bigger problem than hunters on the edge of our territory." Bastian took the metal prongs and crushed the square into tiny pieces. "The first one was a bullet. And this little item"—the debris crumpled and pinged as he dropped it into the metal pan—"appears to be a tracking device. My guess is, her run-in was more than being on the wrong end of fun and games."

Ryker furrowed his brows. "Can they still track it?"

"I don't think so. The chip is destroyed. They won't be able to track the signal," Bastian responded.

Jaw muscles tightening in a moment of silent deliberation, Ryker nodded once. "I'll inform Drew."

"I'll patch her up. I've got my Jeep here. We can get her to my office where I can take better care of her."

"She doesn't get near Drew if there's any risk of them coming after her." The enforcer turned to the brothers. "Why her?"

"I don't know," Seth replied. "I don't think they were hunting wolves. We saw her before she shifted."

"She's a cougar." Ryker stared at her.

"Cougars don't run in packs. They're solitary." Rogue glanced down at her, confusion filling his expression.

"Some. The Goldspark clan is on the other side of the mountain." Ryker shook his head. "I don't think she's one of them."

"Why would she be here then?" Seth pursed his

lips and stared at the slumbering enigma. Why would this incredible creature be all alone in the woods? And when did they put a tracker in her arm? Was it some kind of sick catch-and-release hunt? The pieces didn't add up and dread flooded him. The risk the situation posed to the pack amplified with every question and he couldn't shake off the burden of failure.

"Good question." Bastian nodded.

"Secure her. Find me when she wakes." The enforcer pursed his lips.

"Hey, Doc?" Seth faced Bastian. "When we first tried to pull her out, we both got shocked. Would the tracker have been electrified or something?"

The bowl filled with debris remained on the table. Bastian studied the pieces of the device. "No, but even if it were, it was embedded in her skin. There's no way it could shock you without direct contact."

Seth shook his head. The obscurity of the cougar woman's attempted assassination remained unsolved.

**

14

Terror shot through her as she catapulted for the forest. Griffith followed her. Bullets zinged past her head, and he hollered. She swung around to find her brother on the ground bleeding.

"Run, Klaya, run," he roared.

Klaya bolted upright and screamed, but she wasn't in the forest anymore. She was in a room, surrounded by white, glass-doored cabinets filled with medical supplies. A stabbing pain in her shoulder jarred her, and she collapsed onto her back with a painful thud. She gripped her left forearm, the sting shot up to her shoulder, and grogginess filled her weary head. Perspiration saturated her face and body as the fever burned deep inside her. Parched, she tried to swallow.

"You okay?" A strange voice sounded from the doorway.

"Who the hell are you?" She tried to sit up. Her heart pummeled against her chest as she panted for air.

"It's okay. We're here to help. We found you in the forest." A tall man with dark hair approached her bedside, his hands up in the air. "I swear, I'm not gonna hurt you. My name is Seth."

Something about his deep-brown eyes, however, held a gentle kindness. He didn't look familiar, but he wasn't one of *them*. "Where am I?"

"Los Lobos, in the doctor's office." The stranger—Seth—spun around and headed toward the door but stopped at a water cooler. He tugged a paper cup from the dispenser on the side and poured some water.

"Los Lobos? How did I get here?" She swallowed hard against the dry lump in her throat.

The man returned and handed her the cup. She stared at the water, mulling over the risk of what it may contain, but then slurped it down anyway to quench her thirst.

"My brother, Rogue, and I found you. We brought you here so our friend could help. You got shot."

"Griffith?" Tears welled as flashbacks of him hanging in chains in the cellar flooded back. The horrific torture he'd endured at the hands of their captors, and their relentless efforts to force him to shift. The final moment he told her to run, and the bloody butchery as she escaped, leaving him behind. At first, she'd refused to leave her brother there, but he'd sacrificed himself to save her. There was no

16

other choice; stay and fight at his side and they would both die, or do what he said and run. Instinct took hold. It happened so fast, she didn't have time to regret. Now, he was gone, all because of her.

White-hot tingles of shock radiated through her chest as her memory flooded back and she dropped the empty cup over the edge of the bed. "They killed him." Bursting into tears, she grasped the sheets and clutched them to her chest with trembling fingers.

The man stood beside her, helplessness filling his deep-brown eyes. "I'm so sorry."

The pain overpowered her and darkness took hold.

The cougar slept soundly with shallow breaths as Seth remained seated in the metal chair, watching her with both intense dread for her injuries and fascination with her beauty and the mystery surrounding her arrival. Despite her paleness from her trauma and blood loss, she was exquisite. Luxurious, long, red hair settled around her head and shoulders on the white pillow case .Her porcelain features and sumptuous lips beckoned him. It took every ounce of self-control he had to resist his need for proximity to her. What was this strange compulsion he had to be near her?

"Did she say anything?" Ryker called from the doorway, with Rogue at his side.

Seth approached them and spoke in a low voice. "She said they killed...Griffith?"

"Who is Griffith?" Rogue looked to Ryker.

The enforcer slumped his shoulders with a heavy exhale. "Dammit."

"What is it?"

Ryker turned to leave. "Seth, stay with her in case she wakes up again."

"Is it okay if I come with you?" Rogue pleaded.

"Let's go."

***

The clouds rolled over, and the sky grew dim as Rogue followed Ryker down the road to The Den. Cold rain started to patter down. Rogue knew better than to question the enforcer. The fact he allowed him to tag along was surprise enough.

They ducked inside the bar as the downfall intensified.

"Lovely day, ain't it, gentlemen?" Kayden, the

bartender, wiped the countertop. "Beer?"

Ryker shook his head. "Where's Gee?"

"He's in the kitchen. I'll get him." Kayden headed to the door behind the bar. "Gee, you're wanted out here."

Crashes and clatters resonated out of the kitchen, followed by a few select curses. "Kayden, take care of this...." Gee emerged from the door, wiping his hands on a towel.

"Don't worry, boss. I've got it." Kayden disappeared into the kitchen.

"What?" The six-foot-seven, three hundred pound man made of pure muscle approached the bar.

"We've got a problem." No emotion touched Ryker's tone or his scent. He could have been discussing the weather.

"What's up?"

"Griffith is dead."

"No." The towering bar owner's eyes reddened. His previous cheerful demeanor shifted to a solemn frown. He sighed, resting his forearms on the counter. "When?"

"Today, far as I can tell."

"How?"

"No details. His sister is in Doc's office, shot."

"Who did it?"

"Hunters. Pretty boy here and his bro found her."

Gee glanced to Rogue. "Details?"

Tension filled his jaw and his stomach churned as the visions of her bloodied body rolled through his head. He ground his teeth. "She was being tracked, got shot on the edge of our territory. She had a tracer in her arm."

The brutality these monsters put her through made his blood boil. If there had been a moment to spare at the time they rescued her, he would have hunted the rest down and torn them apart. Those bastards that escaped got off easy.

"Is she gonna live?" The bear arched his brows.

"Bastian thinks so." Rogue shifted his stance. He'd never seen the big guy get emotional over bad news before.

"What did she say?"

"Not much. She's pretty messed up. But the attackers were in camouflage gear, had rifles, and...Seth and I killed four of them."

Gee shook his head. "There were more of them, weren't there?"

"We think maybe three more on-site." Rogue

studied their difficult-to-read expressions. "Who is she? And who was Griffith?" How come he'd never heard of the cougar or her brother before?

The bear straightened. "Join me out back."

Once outside, Gee continued. "When Drew was banished by Magnum and lived outside of the pack, he got to know some other folks. Nonhuman folks. Griffith and his sister, Klaya, were a few of them."

"Her name is Klaya?" The name rolled off his tongue, unique and alluring, just like her. The vision of the mysterious redhead haunted him. Rogue was desperate to learn everything he could about her. A strange need to return to her side clawed at his insides.

"She and Griffith left their clan decades ago and ran solitary. Short story, they saved one of our wolves' lives a few years ago."

"Who did they save?" They'd saved a wolf and he'd never heard of them? Of course, Magnum hadn't been big on sharing, so maybe that was why.

Gee furrowed his brows. "It's not important right now." He exhaled. "They had a little cabin outside our territory, near Keystone."

Who tried to hurt her? Why had they killed her brother and hunted her down like prey? He gritted his teeth, refraining from the surging impulse to slam his palm on the picnic table and demand the answers they avoided giving him. Being a beta was nature's cruel joke on him. His underlying aggression and need to challenge went against the very grain of a less dominant rank in the pack.

Rogue was the protective, impulsive one who acted on instinct first, regardless of the potential consequences. Seth, on the other hand, was the logical brother who deliberated most actions before taking steps. He always needed to seek out direction from their alpha, and even the enforcer. Seth was cut out for the beta role in the pack. One of the hardest lessons Rogue had to learn was to keep his mouth shut and embrace the patience he lacked. A significant genetic abnormality, as far as he was concerned.

"My guess would be the same guys who tried to kill a wolf from our pack years ago." Ryker grumbled.

"What wolf?" The same wolf she and her brother saved? Someone else? "I've never heard this story before."

Gee and the enforcer stared at each other for a moment, as though reading each other's thoughts. Then Ryker shook his head and cleared his throat. "If they tracked her until Doc smashed the chip, they will come looking for her here. She can't be near Drew until it's safe."

"We need to hide her someplace outside of town," Gee agreed.

Ryker nodded.

"Where can we hide her?" Rogue folded his arms.

"There's a cave up in the mountains, Ryker. Amethyst Falls." Gee said. "It's on the edge of Black Hills Territory. You can only get there on foot. It has a freshwater spring inside it, plenty of wild game for food. And it's a good place for healing. If we send provisions, they could hide her there until we get this mess sorted out and are sure there's no risk to the pack."

"They." Rogue lowered his arms. "Who are *they*?" His stomach dropped. Were he and Seth being relegated to babysitting?

Ryker turned with a stern glare. "You and Seth found her. You're responsible for her."

"Come on, you're gonna send us off like fugitives?"

The enforcer let out a quiet growl. "You expect her to stay up there on her own, assuming she can make the trip?"

Rogue pictured the gorgeous redhead. The allure of her scent sparked a sense of adventure deep inside. "You're right, Ryker." Being alone with the mysterious beauty hardly seemed like banishment or even work. It would be a chance to get to know her. What was this strange pull he felt toward her? He wasn't much for spending time in town among the locals anyway. The cave held an intrigue that increased his eagerness to leave, the more he thought about it.

"Remember," the enforcer warned, his voice a cold, deadly rasp, "she's protected and a cougar. Not your latest conquest or your brother's."

The weight of his command slammed against his chest like a ton of bricks. "I get it." Rogue held his palms up in defense. "No funny business." He was known as the town playboy. This woman was different, though. He hadn't even seen her conscious, yet, and concern for her well-being like he'd never experienced before settled in his bones.

"In the meantime," Gee jumped in, "we need to meet with the rest of the pack and prepare for unwanted company, so I'll get to it." He got up and headed inside the bar, followed by more crashes and clunks and a few additional swear words. "Kayden?" he bellowed.

"I've got it, boss," Kayden's muffled voice called out.

No one ever toyed with Gee, but his massive hands and long limbs provided several opportunities over the years for Rogue to razz the big guy. Today was a serious matter. There was no room for banter.

Chapter Three

The cool metal seat offered no solace as Seth sat against the wall. Racked with anxious anticipation, he bit his bottom lip as Bastian lifted open Klaya's left eyelid and inspected her pupil. Worry tightened his chest. What were the chances she would recover from her injuries?

The pack doctor proceeded to remove the bandages from her arm. "Damn, she's a fast healer. Look." He showed Ryker who stood at his side. "Let's check the gunshot." Ryker helped turn her unconscious form onto her side. Bastian covered her hips with the sheet and lifted the hospital gown off her back to snip the bandages off. "She's doing great." He cocked his head. "If I hadn't treated her myself, I would have said this wound happened three weeks ago."

"Will she be able to walk?" Wearing his usual somber expression, Ryker crossed his arms.

"The impact was close to the spine. We'll have to wait until she wakes up again to know for sure, but I'm a betting man, and I'd put my money on her." Bastian smoothed his hand over the forming scar. "No infection. She's lucky."

"I don't know how lucky I'd classify myself," a soft voice replied.

Seth's heart skipped a beat. "She's awake." He abandoned his chair to join them at her bedside, desperate to *see* her. Bright amber eyes held the warmth of the sunrise. Some color had returned to her pale face, and her full luscious lips were a dark, delectable pink compared to the almost white he witnessed when she nearly bled to death. "Hey, Klaya, do you remember me?"

"I got shot in the back, not the head," she grumbled. "Can I lie down again and cover my business?"

Seth stepped away as an ache filled his belly. After slaughtering the hunters and carrying her to safety, he had hoped to gain some favor from the beautiful stranger. It never occurred to him, she would respond with animosity, but, she was injured and alone in a strange place. If he had his way, she would never be alone again.

The dire need to protect her and stay by her side clenched his heart. If only he could make her understand the wild desire. If only he understood it himself. Had he become a blundering idiot over a maiden in distress? Or was this deep-seated need a result of saving her life? None of it made sense.

"Of course." Bastian tucked her gown over her and eased her into place. "How does the wound feel now?"

"Less intense." She rolled her shoulders and cringed. "Still hurts like hell."

"I can give you something for the pain."

"Won't do any good. It'll burn out of my system before it does anything." She waved off the offer.

"Will she be able to walk?" Ryker was relentless. Did the enforcer really need her gone that much?

"She'll need time," Seth interceded. Then, his breath hitched. Why was she sneering at him? Hadn't he just helped her? To rush her out the door before she was healed, and send her on her own would have been callous and risky. How did this suggestion make him the bad guy?

"We're getting to that part soon. The doctor went

to the foot of the bed and pressed the tip of his pen against her the soles of her feet. "We're almost done. Can you feel this?"

"Yeah, I can." She wiggled her toes.

Sensation in the feet was a good sign, wasn't it?

Doc continued to test other parts of her legs. She flinched and gasped.

"Sorry, I want to be sure there are no complications from the wound." He tucked the sheet over her legs.

"I'm not paralyzed, I feel everything," she whispered.

"You need to stay on bed rest for a while before I release you."

"I have nowhere to go." She stared up toward the ceiling. Tears spilled down the sides of her face.

"Klaya, I'm Ryker, Drew's...."

"His enforcer, second in command, I know who you are. And Bastian Storm, the doctor, and the kid over there is Seth," she scoffed.

His heart sank. "Kid?"

"Now we're finished with the introductions, can you all leave me alone for a while?"

"Not yet." He shook his head. "Who did this to you?"

"I don't know who they are." Tears filled her eyes.

The sweetness of her scent shifted. A peppery spike in her pheromones revealed her fear. The pulse behind his ears thrummed and the hair on the back of his neck spiked. He stepped closer to shield her from any more interrogation.

If Ryker picked up on the same cues he had, the enforcer didn't show it. "Where were you when they attacked?"

Klaya's chin quivered. "Our cabin in Keystone."

"What happened to Griffith?" he persisted in his typical cold monotone.

"They shot him," she barked.

Ryker nodded once. "That's it?"

The cougar white-knuckled the cotton sheet draped over her and glowered at Ryker. The rapid beating of her heart echoed in Seth's ears.

"No, first they shot us with tranq darts. When we woke up, they had us chained up in some cellar and they tortured him." She gritted her teeth. "They sliced my arm open and shoved something inside it." She inspected her bandaged forearm. "Before they could do anything else to me, Griffith attacked them to give me a chance to escape. Even though he sacrificed himself, they still tracked me down in the forest. After they shot me, I can't remember anything else."

The enforcer remained silent.

Klaya snarled. "That's it, there's nothing else to tell."

Another nod.

"Where's Drew?" she demanded

"Busy." Ryker headed for the door. With a wave, he motioned Bastian to follow.

Seth lingered on the spot, his heart aching for the pain and suffering she had endured.

"What do you want?" she barked at him.

His stomach churned under her spiteful glare. "Uh, nothing."

"Stop flashing the pity eyes at me and leave me alone." Her chin quivered.

"I'm not, I...." Her bitterness was justified, but her words stung.

"Seth, time to talk," Ryker called from outside. "Allana will stay with her."

Despite the need to remain, he complied with the enforcer's command.

On his way out of the doctor's office, Seth passed Bastian's mate, Allana on her way in. Seth chewed the inside of his lip with frustration. Despite the constant distraction of the unpleasant exchange with the cougar, he tried to shake off his incessant need to shelter her.

He joined the enforcer, Gee, and Rogue at the picnic table behind the bar building and settled on the squeaky wooden bench with weariness. "She's gonna be a handful."

"She's hurt, scared, and in mourning. Being a little aggressive is a sign she hasn't lost her fight." Gee grinned.

"You think she will agree to the cave?" Rogue asked.

"She doesn't have much choice. I imagine being hunted doesn't hold much interest for her. She needs time to heal." Seth traced his thumb over the condensation on his glass of cold water. The icy words from the mysterious redhead stilled weighed heavy on his mind. "Besides, if the tracer was still active when we brought her to the ranger station, it's only a matter of time before they show up here. Hell, they could be here by morning."

"The pack is ready for anyone who comes looking for trouble," Gee piped up. "She's healing fast, so the hike to the cave looks promising. We'll grab what you need at the convenience store. If she can walk, I would say you should leave at first light."

"There's no cell phone service up there," Ryker noted. "It's only reachable on foot, and you'll be out of touch."

"We can handle it."

Ryker nodded. "I'll come up with Drew when we know it's safe."

"What are we supposed to do up there?" Rogue scrubbed his face. "She's pissed. It's gonna be hell."

Not to mention the order to abstain from pursuing the voluptuous feline. I don't know if I have the strength to comply. "Give her time. The last thing she should be right now is alone." Seth nudged his brother's shoulder. Despite the hostile glare and harsh words she shot him, a profound need to protect her festered inside his soul.

"She's not a toy." Ryker glared at them both.

"Got it." Rogue shrugged. Seth side-eyed his brother when he heard the distinct grinding of his teeth. Was his older sibling was as taken by Klaya as he was?

"We know," Seth conceded. "The last thing a grieving cougar on the run for her life would be interested in is hooking up with two younger guys, let alone wolves. We respect the situation. You have my word."

"Your word?" Ryker arched a single brow.

"Are you gonna hold that incident against us for the rest of our lives?" Rogue huffed.

"Which one?" Gee snickered.

"Oh, man," Seth hissed. "Rogue, shut up." His brother's tendency to steer toward mischief and his own incessant need to follow had earned them a tarnished reputation no one in the pack forgot.

"It was only a few women...we were passing through town. We didn't mean...." He paused, swallowed hard, and chugged his water.

"To piss their husbands off? I'm sure you didn't." Ryker's cold tone speared Seth.

"No one got hurt," Rogue fired back then slumped his shoulders.

"Shut up, dude." Seth elbowed him in the ribs. Humiliation and anger enveloped him at his brother's stupidity. Nobody debated with the enforcer.

"Right, because Sam Black needed to replace four tables, three windows, eight chairs, and about four hundred bucks worth of booze for his tavern." Gee folded his arms with a smirk. "It had nothing to do with the bar brawl that ensued after you were caught upstairs in one of his rooms with all four of their wives, right? Or the fact Ryker had to haul himself to Crazy Horse to drag you both home?"

"Right." Seth hung his head and gnashed his teeth. "Not another word, Rogue, or I'll kill you myself."

Gee always threw the lingering shame in their faces. It had been six months and Ryker hadn't trusted them with a single task since—until now. *This is a chance to redeem ourselves in the eyes of the pack, if we don't fuck it up again.* Hooking up with the thirty-somethings in Crazy Horse was Rogue's fine work, and Seth's stupidity in following his big brother's compulsive need for adventure. A fifth of rye hadn't helped their common sense kick in either. The long scar from ten stitches on the back of Seth's skull should serve as a continual reminder not to get caught up in Rogue's playboy antics, but, as fate would have it, the one thing they didn't mind sharing was women.

***

Clad in the jeans, T-shirt, and denim jacket Seth had dropped off for her, Klaya slipped on the hiking boots. The sting in her shoulder intensified as she reached to tighten the second lace. She eased her movements, not eager to repeat the dreadful pain when she'd fastened her bra. Exhaustion saturated her body and mind, to the point numbness had taken every inch of her hostage.

"So," a deep gruff voice called out from the doorway of the doctor's office. "I hear you're stirring up all kinds of trouble, you little minx."

Klaya's throat grew thick at the familiar sound. "Gee?" She fought the sobs filling her chest and stood to greet her old friend. "Griffith's...dead." She shook her head as the words stabbed her heart.

Gee lumbered toward her. "I know. You're safe now, girl. We've got you." He wrapped his bulky arms around her and held her tight as she broke down.

"I couldn't save him...the things they did to him...." Her head spun with grief and terror all at once.

"Hey, listen up," he whispered. "The one thing he always wanted, was for you to be safe. I guarantee if he went down fighting, he wouldn't have had it any other way. You're here now. We're not gonna let anything else happen to you."

"Without him, I'm all alone, Gee. He was the only family I had left."

"We're your family now." Gee was always a security blanket and comrade, as her brother had been. He knew more about her and Griffith than their own people did.

"Where's Drew?" She sniffed back tears and eased out of his embrace.

"You can't see him yet. Ryker notified him."

"Have you come across any others of my Cytaana Clan since we saw you last? Is anyone left?" She searched his face for any sign of hope.

Gee let out a heavy sigh. "I've kept a low profile myself these past years, doll. I haven't strayed far from the Black Hills. Although I haven't heard of any of your clan, I wouldn't rule them out. Survival is the Cytaana strength. Seclusion is their trait. Even if there are any, no one will know unless they seek them out." He stepped back and met her gaze. "Is that what you want? To find your own people?"

Klaya paused. She had no clue what she wanted. "I left over twenty years ago...."

"Right now, the priority is to get you to safety."

What he didn't say told her more. The hunters might still be out there. The thought of the murderous bastards tightened her chest with terror. "I have to leave. I don't want to put the pack at risk."

"It's okay. We have a plan." He nodded with assurance. "Finish suiting up and we'll head to the store for provisions."

"Where am I going?" She shrugged and then cringed at the jolt through her traumatized muscles.

"There's a special place, secluded, safe, and has everything you need to get past this." He flashed a grin. "Trust me, sweetheart. You will get through this."

"You're one of the few people in this pathetic world I do trust, Gee." She tucked her chin down. "And Drew, and Griffith...."

"Hey, don't give up. This place we're sending you to is one I spent some time myself at a critical point in my life. I know it holds the elements you need to be surrounded by right now. It's a perfect place to get your bearings while you work through this. Rogue and Seth may seem like an odd choice as protectors. They're young and impulsive, but they can step up to the plate when needed. They'll fight to the death to keep you safe."

"I believe you, but I don't want anyone else to die because of me."

"No one is going to die, not them, and certainly not you."

38

"Tell me about these two who found me?" Curiosity beat out her need to be morose.

Gee let out a belly laugh before he gave the lowdown. "I give them a hard time, but the brothers are good guys. Rogue, the blond, is the dominant one and the town prankster. He's a little on the impulsive side, but a fierce protector. Seth, the dark-haired one, is the scholar and the follower, a good fighter, loyal and fearless."

"Seth tried to be nice, but I was terrible toward him," she confessed.

"One thing I can tell you about them is they are no strangers to grief and sorrow."

Chapter Four

The hike up the mountain had already taken almost two hours. All three carried jammed backpacks and a duffle bag. The boys had made sure she carried the lightest of the loads to ease her discomfort, but she'd insisted on fending for herself.

The brush was thick, the air crisp, and the conversation nonexistent. Klaya led the way, map in hand, and avoided as much interaction with the brothers as possible. Her body temperature ran hot. She had already tied her jacket to her waist, but her blood nearly boiled from the healing of her wounds.

Not far from their destination, she stopped on the stony ridge framing their path to scan the environment. It was glorious. An endless sea of green treetops topped by intricate rock formations overlooked a small river. She steadied herself to catch a better glimpse of the exquisite scenery. A quick glance over the side and her breath caught in her throat at the sheer drop from the ridge to the rocky water below. A wave of lightheadedness rushed over her, and she teetered on the edge of the rocks and lost her balance.

"Whoa," the boys called in unison.

The heat of hands encased both her arms, pulling her to safety in mid-fall. A jolt of energy sent a sharp sting to her biceps.

"Ouch," she snarled and tugged out of their grasp.

"Are you okay?" Seth asked.

"What the hell was that?" She stared at their hands.

"It's the second time it happened." The brown of his eyes intensified with his confusion.

"What do you mean the second time?"

"When we pulled you from the tree, we got a shock, exactly like this," the one on the left continued with crinkled brows.

"You did?" She gasped. *Oh, crap The Nasc? This can't be right. They're wolves, and I'm a cougar. It can't be possible?*

"What was it?" Seth asked.

41

"Nothing," she snapped. "Ever heard of static electricity?" She massaged her tingling skin, unwilling to divulge the truth behind the transfer of energy, or the continual warmth coursing through her veins. *It has to be nothing. What the hell is happening to me?*

"Do you need to rest?" the sandy blond with shaggy curls interrogated, concern fanning from his dark-green eyes.

"I'm fine," she growled. Another bout of dizziness struck her and her knees gave out. They caught her as she dropped to the ground.

"Listen." They squatted beside her as the brown-eyed brother spoke. "You've been pushing yourself really hard. There's no rush to get to the middle of nowhere."

"Seth, right?"

"Yeah, I'm Seth, he's Rogue."

"Charmed, I'm sure." She snagged her water bottle off the side clip of her backpack and took a long fortifying swig. "Don't treat me like some lame victim."

"We meant no disrespect. Let's slow down for a minute, ok?" Seth pleaded. "You've out-walked me; my legs are cramped up." He winked and patted his upper thigh.

Klaya spied the kindness in his eyes. On any other day, the warmth of those chocolate-brown orbs would have made her swoon. "Whatever. Take a load off, kids."

Seth's cheeks brightened to a remarkable shade of red. "That's the second time you've called me a kid, Klaya. Care to enlighten me why?" He cocked his head.

She scoffed, "What are you guys, like, eighteen?"

Rogue chuckled. "Not exactly, I'm thirty-four. My brother here is thirty-five."

"Baby faces." She did a double take with both of them. "Got any ID to support your claim?"

"The wolf genes keep our stunning good looks a long time." Rogue slapped his leg with amusement.

"I'm guessing you're not twenty-nine then?" Seth arched his brows and inquired with caution.

"Smart boy, never ask an older woman her age."

"It's cool. I wouldn't put you past twenty-nine." He smiled.

"I'm forty-five." She cracked a grin. "But thank you for lying about my appearance."

"You do not look forty-five." Rogue plopped down on the ground beside her.

43

"Cougars age slower, too."

"How is your wound?" Seth motioned behind her.

She slipped the straps of the pack off her shoulders and stretched. A dull sting splayed the width of her upper torso. "Still hurts, but getting better every hour."

"I've never seen anyone heal so fast." Rogue grabbed his water and tossed back a mouthful. "Is it a cougar thing?"

"I take it you haven't had much experience with the Cytaana Clan before?"

"No, you're the first I've met, well"—Seth glanced to his brother—"we've met."

"I'll likely be the last." She narrowed her eyes and tipped her head back with a sigh.

"What do you mean?"

"I mean, we've been getting knocked off one at a time over the years. I don't think there's anyone left but me."

Klaya sat in awkward silence with the brothers. The torment of how much they knew about her was more than she could bear. What she wouldn't give for a way to erase the last forty-eight hours and everything they had learned about her. The last thing she wanted or needed was to be viewed as a victim, for anyone to know her trauma. She was no victim, but she was broken, in every sense of the word. Nothing would ever be the same again, but this was her baggage to drag with her, and she had no desire to allow anyone even the slightest glimpse of her despair.

***

The arrival at the cave was a welcome one. Rogue walked behind Klaya and his brother and snagged a branch of pine. He swept their tracks from the dirt and scattered forest debris to hide any sign of their direction. The blisters on his feet were killing him. He hated wearing shoes, hell, he hated clothes, but, given the circumstances, necessity prevailed.

"I'll go ahead and scout out the cave." He pulled out his flashlight and clicked it on.

"No you won't. I'm not a helpless damsel in distress." Klaya tugged out her own flashlight and led the way.

"She's a handful," he whispered to Seth.

"I heard that."

"You know"—he trotted behind her and Seth

followed—"I gotta admit, this whole independent thing is cool, but we're starting to feel a little emasculated here. Can you work with us, please?"

Klaya halted and spun around. "You're right. I'm sorry." Her voice quaked.

"Hey." Seth stepped forward. "Are you okay?"

Rogue's flashlight beam lit up her tear-filled eyes.

"I don't mean to be a bitch. I'm not usually so cold...." Her chin quivered.

"You lost your brother, you're all alone, and you're scared?" Seth interjected.

"Scared, yes, but not for myself." She nodded. "Neither of you guys wants to be stuck up here in the middle of nowhere with me. And, if they find us, you could both get—"

"Hey." Rogue brushed a tear off her cheek with the pad of his thumb. "You got the two bad-ass brothers here to keep you safe. We won't let anything happen to you. We promised to protect you, and we'll gladly give our lives to do it." Heat filled his belly at the simple touch of her skin under his finger.

"That's the point. I don't want anyone else to die because of me, not Griffith, not you two, not Drew or any of your pack. Part of me wants to track those bastards down and take them out. I don't care if I die doing it."

A brief moment of awkward silence passed. It was too much for Rogue to bear. "But you'd miss out on our devious charm, Klaya." He grinned. "I brought Battleship, a deck of cards, and dice. We're gonna have a blast."

Klaya burst into tear-filled laughter. She swiped the wetness off her cheeks with the back of her hand. "Thank you." She stood on her tippy-toes and kissed him on the cheek then faced Seth and did the same. "You're both very sweet."

"We promise no more harm will come to you." Rogue cupped his cheek where she had kissed him. An incredible hunger swept over his lower torso. How could a tiny kiss on the cheek make his loins ache?

With a deep inhale, she forced a grin. "Let's see what adventure lies inside here, shall we, boys?" Klaya gestured ahead and let them take the lead.

"We came up here when we were kids. From what I remember, there's an indoor waterfall and a ready-made tub. The water a little chilly, but after a while you don't notice."

"Whoa." Klaya paused and inspected the rock walls with her flashlight and her fingertips.

"Amethyst, this is so beautiful." She shone the light across the wall and the pointed clusters of purple and white glittered all around.

"If we continue a little farther in, we get to the center of the cave. It's inside the mountain, but with the waterfall and high ceiling, we can build a fire in here." Seth moved faster ahead.

"Yeah, I remember now," Rogue recollected with bitter sweetness. "We hid up here after we crashed Dad's pickup truck. We thought for sure he was gonna kill us."

"You crashed his truck?" She gripped Rogue's arm. Her touch warmed his skin. "Did you guys get hurt?"

"No, other than our pride. We were trying to show off...." He cleared his throat and glanced away from her alluring cognac eyes.

"For some girls?" she pried.

"Yeah, we were twelve and thirteen. The old man was pissed, but Mom was so scared for us. When Dad found us and dragged us home, we were stunned because he just dropped the subject."

Seth chuckled. "Man, we got off easy. Pops could tan the hide of a rodeo bull if he was mad enough."

"Your parents, Gee mentioned...uh...."

A shockwave of grief rushed through his chest.

"How did they...?" Klaya softened her voice. "I'm sorry."

The need to shed tears thickened Rogue's throat. He swallowed hard. "Don't be. It's fine."

"Do you mind me asking what happened to them?"

"We don't know much." Seth exhaled a heavy breath.

Klaya glanced back and forth between them with raised brows. "It's okay if you don't...."

Seth cleared his throat. "Our folks moved us out of town ages ago when Magnum was alpha because he went crazy. None of us wanted to be under his reign. We found a small cabin past Keystone and moved us there until Drew became alpha. Our parents stayed at the cabin, but we returned to Los Lobos."

Rogue's stomach knotted as his brother babbled on. Did she really need to hear their sob story? After all, they were sent to protect her, this wasn't about them. Rogue wanted to launch his fist into his brother's gut right now to shut him up.

"Last fall," Seth continued, "we took some work out of state for a few weeks. Drew told us he'd have someone from the pack check on our folks to make sure they had supplies and stuff while we were gone. When we returned to town, he and Ryker met us at Gee's bar to tell us." Seth shook his head.

"We don't know who or why, but someone broke into their place. They took Mom, and Dad...." Rogue's chest tightened, squeezing the air from his lungs.

Klaya stared blankly at him. "What did they do to them?"

A heat wave of rage crashed over his chest. "They killed them." Rogue growled and pushed past his brother and Klaya.

Chapter Five

The center of the cave was massive, exactly as the guys had described. There was a slim cascading waterfall about twenty feet high, and the spilling water collected into a deep stone crevice in the ground, creating an ideal pool area, big enough for ten people to swim. Above the waterfall a circular opening in the stone ceiling spilled enough sunlight through to illuminate the surrounding area. Spectacular clusters of purple and white crystals protruded from the surrounding rock walls.

"Welcome to Amethyst Falls."

"This is incredible. I almost feel guilty calling it a hideout. People would pay money to stay here." Klaya glanced over to Rogue, still rattled by his shift in mood when they arrived.

Blondie tossed his bag on the ground and

scouted around the interior of the cave. The scent of leathery musk she had grown to associate with him emitted a slight sourness now. His tense shoulders vibrated with energy as he skulked around the cave.

Seth plopped down on his sleeping bag and pulled his boots off. "Hey, don't mind Rogue. He can come off as a little uptight with some issues, but he'll calm down soon."

"Okay." She forced a grin.

"Gee says this is the perfect environment for healing."

"Why is that?"

"See right up there?" He motioned to the ceiling. "Tonight you'll see the light of the full moon through the opening. Those clusters of gemstones you've been admiring?" He pointed to the walls.

"Yes?"

"They have healing energies associated with earth. The mountain also contains deposits of rock salt. Now, picture the power of the moon lighting up the energy of the stones surrounded by the cleansing and protection of pure salt. You're in the middle of a ready-made healing circle."

"Salt, huh? It's incredible." She tried to hold back her smile of amusement at a wolf tutoring her about healing properties of rock and minerals. If only he knew of her upbringing.

"I'm going out to grab some firewood." Rogue dropped his bag and headed down the tunnel.

"Do you want help?" Klaya called after him.

"No." His voice was cold.

She sat for a moment and glanced over to Seth. "Did I upset him?"

He sighed and shook his head. "Our parents' death seems to spike his rage more so than mine, most times."

"How long ago did they die?"

"About nine months ago."

"I take it they did more to your parents than shoot them?"

"Yeah, I mean Drew didn't give us all the details, but what we did learn was horrific. No one should have to die like that."

"And you never learned who did it or why?"

"No. There have been a number of *disappearances* over the years and more than a few bodies. At first, we suspected Magnum or his thugs, but we had no proof, no evidence to verify either way. To be honest, we don't know what ties them all together."

"I can appreciate the rage it fills you both with." More than she could convey with mere words.

"Look, I know it's still really raw for you, Klaya, and I won't push, but if you need to talk about what happened to you and your brother, I'm a pretty good listener."

At his prompt, violent images flooded her brain of how they tortured Griffith while she was forced her to watch. "I'm not ready yet." She trembled with fear.

"I know, but I'm here when you are."

"Thanks, Seth." The idea she'd triggered Rogue's upset left her with a great deal of unease. "I'm gonna go see if I can help bring in some wood." She got up.

"I'll come, too." He grabbed his boots.

"No, it's fine. Take a load off, I won't be long." She grabbed her flashlight and headed out through the tunnel.

At the entrance of the cave, Klaya listened for the sound of movement, any movement. Her keen senses had been off since the attack, but she took a long whiff and tried to locate Rogue's scent. A sudden hint of the familiar leather and musk she had come to associate with him crept up her nose. A magnetic draw to the aroma guided her to the right. She traipsed down the wooded path along the side of the cave and listened. The scent grew stronger as she moved forward, but the lack of sound troubled her. She halted, her tummy tensed, and the hair on the back of her neck prickling. No birds, no wildlife, not one forest creature moved.

She inhaled again, this time, frozen with fear. A second scent—one of gun oil and burnt cigar. A smell she was painfully familiar with. Klaya inched her way to the nearest tree. Rogue's cologne grew stronger, but, still, there was no sound. She clung to the trunk and glanced around.

A hand gripped her arm and intense heat rushed over her skin. She gasped. Another hand covered her mouth, and she struggled to break free.

"Shhh, it's me," Rogue whispered into her ear.

The heat filled with tingles from his touch surprised her. She relaxed and he let go. He pointed to the right where she caught a glimpse of a shadow moving deep in the forest.

Klaya glanced up the tree. Rogue nodded. She gripped the low branches and climbed the massive trunk with her catlike skills. Rogue climbed the opposite side. They ascended thirty feet and scouted the forest.

"I could only find two of them," he murmured.

"One headed east." He pointed the direction headed away from the cave. "The second is about twenty yards from here."

"If they are scouting, they don't know we are here. If we attack, there will be more coming in from behind. We have no way to let Seth know." She bit her lip.

"For now, we watch and see."

Klaya agreed and settled on a solid branch. They took turns glancing around. Her breath hitched. The gunman below moved three trees over from where they were hiding. Her acute hearing picked up radio static. "I can hear them."

"I can, too."

"There's no sign of anyone here. The tracks ended by the forest, a hundred yards back. Over."

"Head to base. There's no signal on her tracer."

"Copy that." The man below walked past their tree and paused. He held his rifle and slowly twisted around, spying through the scope.

"Tin man, let's go." The radio crackled.

"Roger that." He darted toward the east.

"We wait awhile longer," Rogue whispered.

They scouted the length of the forest. The bristling hair on the back of her neck settled. A robin

56

perched on the branch above them and she exhaled with relief. "They're gone."

"Yeah, they're lucky I didn't tear them apart."

Klaya caught his wandering glare in the direction the assassins left. His cheeks darkened as he flexed his jaw muscles. *Wow, he has a real hate on for them. Is it because of me?* It didn't seem likely, but the Nasc—the jolt she felt from them was the distinct protective energy that happens with destined mates.

"How come they didn't find our tracks?"

"The first thirty feet or so is all stone, so there were no tracks. I took some branches and swiped away the footprints we left from the edge of the forest."

"Very clever." He was smart and ruggedly handsome, too. She melted under the captivating gaze of his vibrant emerald orbs and a tickle shimmied down her spine. Each moment she spent with Rogue and his brother, they got a little deeper under her skin.

"We've had some practice hiding out." He winked.

"I'll bet. The two of you seem to have a reputation for getting into trouble." She prodded.

"You could say that."

"I just did."

Rogue's grin shifted to a frown when their gazes collided.

"I was only teasing." She reached over and patted his hand.

"I know." He pressed his lips tight. "Let's get inside and update Seth."

They descended the tree.

"What if they decide to search the cave?"

Rogue glanced around them. "They didn't find anything, there's no reason to think they'll return any time soon, but we'll be ready for them."

Chapter Six

Glorious pink and orange streams of the sunset light poured through the hole in the ceiling. The trio had worked together gathering stones, wood, and kindling and had lit a cozy fire off the side of the pool.

The boys began to strip their clothes off.

Klaya widened her eyes. "Excuse me, what do you two think you're doing?"

"Sorry, habit." Rogue chuckled. "We're gonna shift to catch some food for dinner."

"Oh." Her cheeks burned. "I could help."

"No, you're still healing. We've got this. It's the masculine thing to do. We have to prove ourselves, don't we?" Seth cracked a grin.

"By all means." She covered her eyes while they discarded the rest of their clothing.

Warmth curled around her spine at the thought

of them disrobing mere feet away from her. The temptation to peek proved too much to handle. She still actively mourned her big brother. Surely peeping at hot young wolves would be the last thing on her mind, but their captivating scents overpowered her grief.

Through the tiny spaces between her fingers, she caught a breathtaking glimpse of two virile, defined, taut bodies. Although their hair and faces were in direct contrast of one another, one fair, the other dark, each held unique, handsome, and rugged features. They both possessed identical flawless, bronzed skin with lean muscles. The wolves showcased broad shoulders, solid pectorals, and chiseled arms a girl would love to be cradled in. With their washboard abs, tight asses, and powerful legs, these two were built for speed and stamina and would make an ideal meat sandwich for any lucky lady. The vision of their two thick, extended cocks triggered a longing deep inside. Klaya licked her lips; her inner cougar clawed to pounce.

She squinted her eyes shut as a wave of shame washed over her, but, then, a compelling sound of grunts and groans forced them open again. Klaya removed her hand and stared in amazement when both men dropped onto their hands and knees to transform. She had witnessed Griffith over the years, but his shift into a cougar was profoundly different, far faster and simpler.

They braced themselves as their magnificent bodies morphed. Their faces contorted, fur grew, and claws spiked out of their fingertips. Within seconds, they towered before her. Brown eyes shifted into a chocolate-colored wolf, with a white patch over his left eye and another in the shape of a diamond centered on his chest. Rogue transformed into a sandy-blond wolf with black patches all over his fur. More ebony surrounded his eyes, like the mask of a thief in the night. They were spectacular. Both wolves watched her with intensity. She smiled, and they bolted out the tunnel.

The lingering desire was next to impossible to dispel. "Heaven help me. I can't believe I could even entertain the thought of a man right now, let alone two." A tear spilled down her cheek.

Then recollection of showering shards of glass came crashing back. "I can't. I'm not ready yet. Not to deal with this and not to move on." Klaya brought her knees to her chest, cradled her arms on top, and sobbed. A cry long since overdue, she was grateful for the time alone to finally let it out.

After a much-needed hour or so to herself, she was able to have her emotional letdown and unpack her backpack. She had brought a stack of candles, matches, clothes from the secondhand store in town, and some plates to eat from. Each of their bags contained bare essentials for their time in seclusion. Now, she had to wait for the boys to return.

***

"Although I'm not partial to rabbit, you guys did a great job. It's pretty tender."

"Cougars have preference in wild game?" Rogue snickered.

"Actually, I'm vegan," she retorted.

"Are you kidding me?" Seth dropped his plate. "I'm so sorry."

"I'm just fucking with you." She burst into laughter. "I couldn't be vegan if my life depended on it. I'm a total carnivore."

"So, what's your poison?" Rogue stuffed the last of his sizzling bunny into his mouth.

"I could kill for some venison right now." She licked her lips.

"Order for tomorrow?" Seth nodded.

"Sure."

Klaya glanced up at the ceiling. The pinks and oranges had dissipated. Rays of dark purple and streams of moonlight took their place.

"I think Gee is wiser than anyone gives him credit for."

"Why?" Brown eyes piped up.

"He sent us here to a place of healing and protection. My clan, the Cytaana, are an ancient Celtic clan of cougars. Griffith and I left when we were in our twenties, after our parents died.

"So, you're an orphan, too?" Rogue stared at the fire, the corners of his lips curled downward.

"I am," she murmured.

"How did they die?" Seth piped up.

"The alpha of the clan killed them." She averted her gaze from theirs, hesitant to confess their fate.

"Your own alpha?" Rogue rasped.

"He went mad. He killed many in our clan. That was why Griffith and I fled in the middle of the night. We heard, years ago, the alpha met an untimely demise after crossing paths with a coyote pack."

"Sounds brutal," Seth whispered.

Klaya caught their widened eyes and dropped

jaws.

"In my mind, the vicious death was karma catching up to him. There's no love lost on my part. I never had any use for an alpha after that."

"So, how do you know Drew?" Rogue asked.

"Griffith and I met him in Utah. He was down on his luck. He and my brother became good friends. He stayed with us for a few months until he said it was time to move on." She grabbed a stick and poked at the glowing red embers of the fire. "He was the reason I was headed for Los Lobos when you found me."

"He was?" Seth watched her with knitted brows. "Why?"

"Griffith and I didn't keep in touch, but we caught wind of Magnum's death and heard Drew had become alpha. My brother said if we ran into trouble, we could ask him for help."

Unwilling to relive another trauma, Klaya got up and began hauling the load of firewood she and Rogue left wrapped in the sheet at the edge of the cave.

"Leave it, Klaya. We have enough wood right now," Seth insisted.

"I like to keep busy." She twisted sideways as she

tugged on the load.

A sudden white-hot sting encased Klaya's left shoulder. She winced and dropped to her knees. Perspiration broke out on her face and neck, and she panted.

"Klaya?" Rogue scrambled over to her. "What's wrong?"

Seth placed his cool palm on her forehead then cheek. "You're burning up."

"I'm in healing mode again. It's the gunshot. I strained it when I twisted. I need to lie down."

She hobbled over to the makeshift bed by the fire. Rogue and Seth supported her under the arms.

"Is there anything we should do?" Seth's voice faded in her ears. Klaya dropped to her knees and eased down onto the blanket, searing pain spreading throughout her spine and along her limbs. She closed her eyes. "Let me sleep. I'll be fine."

Chapter Seven

"She's been out a long time. Shouldn't we wake her? Make sure she's okay?" Seth tucked his coat over her shoulder as she lay on her side three feet from the fire.

"She said she needs to sleep."

"I know. I hate seeing her in pain." He stared at the sleeping beauty, the need to cradle her in his arms overwhelming.

"Me, too," Rogue concurred. "She'll be fine. She's wiped out."

A tendril of copper hair clung to her moist forehead. Seth brushed it behind her ear. Searing heat filled the pads of his fingers, and he gasped. "She's burning up."

Rogue glanced down at her. "Remember when we found her in the forest? She was burning up then, too."

"Yeah?"

"She was healing then, and you told me she mentioned to Doc in the office when she woke up that pain killers would burn out of her system before they would help. She runs hot in healing mode."

Rogue was never the type to coddle someone when they were sick or injured. A lesson he learned many times over his childhood. The broken arm he suffered when he fell from the tall oak tree in the backyard was met by Rogue's brash response to "shake it off."

A profound need to protect her had taken hold the moment they spotted her in the forest that fateful day, and with every passing moment, it intensified. He imagined it was the same for Rogue, given how close he sat to her, and watched over her. Seth was the touchy-feely one, whereas Rogue tended to guard from afar. It amazed Seth sometimes how his brother made very little effort for any body contact with others. With the exception of getting randy with women who caught his attention. There was always a means to an end with Rogue, but Seth had a deep-seated need to display affection with physical touch.

"She's so beautiful," Rogue whispered.

He snapped his head up and stared at his brother with surprise. "Yeah, she is."

"What?"

"Nothing, it's...." Seth chose his words carefully. "You never talk like that about chicks you're into. You tend to go straight for the gold. Flattery is not your thing."

"Klaya is no chick," he protested softly. "She's...."

"Incredible," Seth finished his thought.

"Exactly."

"And, as Ryker made very clear, she's off-limits."

"I know." Rogue shrugged with a frown. "Her scent drives me wild, though."

"I hear ya," Seth concurred. "It's intoxicating."

"It's gonna be a tough week." Rogue twisted side to side and adjusted his pants.

"Dude?"

"Not my fault, involuntary." He scampered to his feet and headed to the waterfall. "Time for a cold shower."

"I can hold off. Go ahead." Seth chuckled.

In truth, he needed one as badly as Rogue did, but he had no desire to leave her side. Conflicted with worry and longing, he needed to stay with her until she awoke.

Chapter Eight

The dawn light streamed through the stone ceiling and caressed Klaya's cheek. Warmth crept over her skin with an enjoyable prickling. The constant but calming splatter of water echoed through the air. She stretched and yawned as she rolled over, but bumped into something at her side. She opened her eyes and bolted up. She found the rugged blond curled up on his side facing her, on her left and the brown-eyed wonder curled up on her right. Both were sound asleep. Each brother sported luscious lips she wanted to taste. Rogue's mass of thick blond curls, she wanted to run her fingers through. Seth's straight black hair, she wanted to smooth her palm along. She could easily remain tucked between these two day and night.

Reality came crashing in. Griffith, the brutal

attack, the hunters.... *It's morning? How long have I been out?*

A profound sense of safety enveloped her, as did an obsessive need to remain snuggled up next to the young wolves. Was she at this again? The deadened loneliness in her heart seemed to have lifted. An impulse to trace her fingers along the masculine contours of Brown eyes' face took hold. Primal urge compelled her, but common sense prevailed. "What the hell is happening to me?" She glanced to her other side, where Rogue, the handsome blond, rested peacefully. Her inner cougar pined to taste his luscious lips, and nip at the taut flesh of his shoulder.

Parched, she shook her head to dispel the longing and struggled to regain her focus. Water, she had heard water. The cascading falls beckoned her. She inched her way out from between the brothers and headed over to the cool pond. She scooped a handful and drank it up, however, the sweet nectar barely moistened her crusty mouth. She was on the cusp of dehydration. She glanced to her slumbering cave mates. Sure they were still sound asleep, she slipped out of her jeans, T-shirt, and undergarments, and she stepped in. Refreshment washed over her, after the initial shock of the cold. She sucked in a deep breath and dove into the pool. She swam peacefully and headed to the cascading falls. She sat under the spray and allowed the weight of the water wash away her fatigue.

"Good morning, beautiful," a voice called out.

Klaya gasped, and covered her exposed breasts. "Uh, good morning." She glanced over to find both wolves at the edge of the water, sporting naughty smiles.

"Don't worry." Seth chuckled and slapped his brother's arm. "We won't peek."

"Speak for yourself." Rogue's penetrating gaze lingered and caused a stir deep inside Klaya's core.

"Stop it." Seth cuffed him in the back of the head and they both spun around to grant her privacy.

Klaya's heart pounded. "Thank you." She swam over and stopped at the edge. "I didn't think this out very well." She could easily climb up the chiseled rock steps, but her clothes lay some distance away.

"That's why we brought you a blanket." Rogue held the gray material up at his side with the other hand clamped over his eyes. "Still not looking, I swear."

Would they look? Or, more importantly, did she want them to? Uncertain, but mildly entertained by his repartee, she climbed out of the water, humiliation saturated her. "Again, thanks." She snatched up the blanket and wrapped it around herself. "All covered up."

"We didn't mean to surprise you." Seth turned around with crinkled brows. "We're glad to see you up and about."

"How long was I out?"

"The whole night."

"Talk about embarrassing." Unconscious and vulnerable were two things she never liked to be.

"No need. We thought it might be awhile." Seth held his leather jacket in his hand and slipped it around her shoulders. "The water is pretty cold; we should get the fire built up."

"A warm fire would be nice," she offered through chattering teeth.

"You must be starving." Seth said.

"Now that you mention it, I am."

"You dry off and get dressed. We have a surprise for you."

"Oh?"

Next to the blazing fire, Klaya snuggled under the extra blankets and happily gobbled up the

72

steaming meat. "I can't believe you caught venison for me." She devoured it as though she had been starved for a week.

"We needed to keep ourselves busy. Old Seth here was driving us both crazy with worry."

"About what?" Her shoulders tensed. "Did the hunters return?"

"No, he was worried about you," Rogue teased and punched his brother in the arm.

"We both were." Seth gnashed his teeth at Rogue then faced her.

Klaya closed her eyes and absorbed the energy around them. A blissful calm resonated through her body. She opened her eyes with relief. "I feel safe. I've never experienced anything quite so powerful before. It must be this cave, it's vibrating with energy."

"Klaya, forgive me for asking, but, what happened to you and your brother?" Rogue's voice softened.

"Dude?" Seth smacked his arm with a tsk. "She told Ryker enough."

"No, it's okay, I should talk about it, or at least try to." She put her plate down and sat cross-legged facing the wolves.

"Only if you feel ready." Tenderness filled Seth's

eyes.

"The truth is, we had been out at the cabin for so long, with no problems, the attack took us by surprise." Her chin quivered at the thought she could have saved Griffith's life.

"It's okay, you don't have to talk about it," Rogue conceded.

"I do." She patted his thigh. "Not too long after we left, our clan had scattered to the forests. We were being hunted."

"By what?"

"First, by our alpha, but, after he died, others were hunted by humans. We never knew who or why. We found a place out in Keystone and settled on new territory. We heard over the years, the clan had died off. Some disappeared, others were murdered, but we never found anyone who could tell us what happened."

She stared at the fire as her thoughts slipped into the past.

"Gee mentioned you and your brother saved a wolf from our pack before?" Rogue watched her.

"We did."

"Who was it?" he persisted.

"We never knew his name." The recall of his

beaten face and mangled body was a cruelty she didn't care to relive. "We wandered outside of the Black Hills territory, trying to find a remote place, free of the scent of humans." She shook her head to dispel the gnawing recollection of gun oil and tobacco scent. "One night, when we were on a hunt for food, we heard men tracking through the forest. They wore combat clothes and carried rifles. They were chasing something."

Klaya slammed her eyes shut and sucked in a sharp breath. She pushed the brutal images aside so she could continue. "They had captured a man. They were doing horrible things to him. They had him chained, they used a cattle prod to torment him."

"Why?"

"They're sadistic bastards." She shrugged and grimaced. "Sometimes I wish I understood their motives, but the truth is it doesn't matter."

"What happened to the man?"

"They put a tracer in his arm and finally made him shift. Then they set him free. The pricks were tracking him down for the fun of it. We found the device in his arm afterward and had to pull it out of his flesh."

"Like you?" Seth let out a low growl.

A shiver snaked along her spine. "Yes, exactly like me...and...."

"You don't have to, Klaya," Rogue cautioned.

The heat of burgeoning tears filled her eyes. "I need to." She sniffled through the dribble of grief seeping from her nose. "Griffith and I attacked the hunters and killed them. It was easy. They weren't aware of us. The wolf was limping and couldn't run. Once the men were dead, we shifted to show him he was safe. I was amazed, he didn't seem surprised that we were cougars. We got him to our cabin. The only thing he would tell us was that he was a friend of Gee's. I sent word for him to come and help. We've known Gee for years...."

"Are you ready to talk about when we found you?" Rogue prodded carefully.

"I am." She expelled a shaky sigh. "It was early morning; we had finished a long night's hunt. We were exhausted." She swallowed hard past the lump in her throat. "I drifted off to sleep until the sounds of shattering glass and gunshots rang through the air." She sucked in a shaky breath, determined not to break down. Seth grasped her hand; his touch sent an instant peace throughout her mind and body. Rogue gave a slight nod of encouragement.

76

She continued, "Griffith ran into my room to protect me. More gunshots littered the air, and pings of wood and plaster scattered down over us from the impact against the ceiling and walls. He said we had to get to the cellar trap door in the kitchen." The words poured out; the images flashed through her brain like a movie in fast motion.

"He told me to run. I took off through the open bedroom door down the hallway leading to the kitchen. When I got there, I spotted a shadow of someone lurking behind the curtain of the open window above the sink." Her stomach tensed. "I grabbed the wooden chair when I saw the barrel of a gun poke through the curtains. I snuck up to the side and slammed the chair through the window. A gunshot zinged past my head and the person dropped with a thud outside."

She couldn't swallow past the lump in her throat, but it was too late to stop. She had to say it out loud, for the first time since it happened. "I shoved the table over and pulled open the trap door in the floor. Griffith raced in after me and we ran down the wooden ladder and rushed toward the doors of the storm cellar which led to outside. Sunlight peered through the cracks." The brief image slowed in her mind, the single moment of hope, and calm before all hell broke loose. "Griffith peered out the cracks of the door; there was movement upstairs. We couldn't tell how many of them there were. He told me, if we get separated, to get my ass to Los Lobos. We propped the door open, scrambled up the concrete steps, and fled into the cover of the nearby forest."

Heated tears spilled down her cheeks. The images burned bright in her brain as she relived the horrible event. "More gunfire rang out behind us. *Faster*, he yelled. I bolted through the opening of the trees and kept going. Griffith was close behind." Terror shot through her as she recited the last moments. "Then, he hollered and I stopped and swung around to find my brother on the ground, bleeding. 'Run, Klaya, run,' he roared." Klaya stopped. Her lungs ached with sorrow as she tried to exhale. Her hands shook, and her heart raced.

After a moment of silence, she tried to compose her racing thoughts. "He told me to keep going, but I...." She fought the vicious surge of grief to no avail. She sobbed as she tried to force the rest of the words out. "I couldn't...."

"You couldn't leave him there." Seth inched closer and cradled her cheek in the heat of his palm.

"No." She trembled. "I tried to pull him into the forest, I begged him to shift."

"Was he...?" Seth winced.

"He was still alive, in terrible pain. The fear in his eyes was unbearable. I was kneeling at his side and a sharp sting pierced my neck. The next thing I remember, I was huddled in a corner," she growled. "I don't know where we were, some basement with concrete walls and no windows. There was a set of stairs leading up to a door. It reeked of death. Blood splatters all over the walls. The stench of must and shit stung my nose. Other cougars' scents littered the whole place."

"There were others?" Seth whispered.

"They had Griffith strung up by the arms; they were beating him, slicing him. They—" She lost the ability to breathe and gasped for air. "They...they...." Klaya shook.

"Hey, it's okay. You're safe now." Rogue inched closer and scooped her up into his arms. He settled her into his lap and cradled her while she broke down.

Seth, right at his side, caressed her face, and whispered, "We're here, Klaya. We've got you."

"We get the picture. You don't have to finish."

Rogue kissed her forehead and held her tight.

"They took their time." She mustered her remaining strength, desperate to get it out. "One held me from behind, another, at my side, forced my eyes open with his fingers. They made me watch every evil thing they did to him. I can still hear his voice, his screams." A bizarre calm washed over her. Numbness filled her limbs and her face. She lost all physical strength and her voice was barely a murmur. "I don't know how long it lasted, but he finally gasped through bloody lips, 'I love you, Klaya. Run. Run fast and don't stop.' He closed his eyes and went still."

The brothers remained silent. Klaya placed her hands on Rogue's chest, pushed herself up, and climbed out of his lap. She left the wolves sitting on the ground and paced around the fire. "The bastard who held me laughed in my ear. The second let go of my face and grabbed my arm." She held up her left forearm where the fresh scar remained. "They sliced me with a knife and jammed something inside my skin. I tried to fight, but they held me until he was finished. Then, they started to jab me with the cattle prod."

Klaya glanced over to find the brothers side by side, their gazes locked on her. "They poked at me, like they did to the wolf we saved, and yelled and hollered. Some laughed—there were maybe ten of them. They wanted me to shift, maybe because Griffith refused to, I don't know. I wasn't gonna give them the satisfaction." She curled her lips. "I knew something they didn't."

"What?" the brothers whispered.

"I could still hear Griffith's heartbeat." A cackle slipped out of her mouth. "They were all focused on the helpless cougar in the corner, and Griffith slipped out of the chains behind them. He shifted and took three of the bastards out before they knew what hit 'em." Klaya wrapped her arms around herself to ward off the shivers of despair. "He roared at me to run. We both knew he wasn't going to make it out of there alive. He took out another one and I bolted for stairs. I don't remember much afterward, I ran fast and hard. I shifted, and there were shots all around me. I remember a stabbing pain in my shoulder, and I dropped to my belly."

"That's when we saw you on the run," Seth piped up. "On the edge of our territory."

"The rest is a haze." She shook her head.

"You crawled to a large oak tree and burrowed your way inside. We ran to you and found the hunters ready to shoot you down. You shifted after you hid."

"I passed out."

Rogue chimed in. "We took four of them out, but there were more."

"I'm sure there were," she scoffed.

"Did any of them talk about what they wanted?" Seth asked.

"They were too busy shouting and laughing. It was a sick game for them," she snarled.

"With assault rifles and tracking devices, Doc thinks this was a high-tech hunt." Brown eyes arched his brows.

"Hold on." Rogue stood up. "You said you smelled death in there?"

"I did." She shivered at the memory.

"And other cougars?"

The rancid memory filled her palate, much to her distaste. "Among other scents, but, yes, it was distinctive."

"Could you place any of the other scents?" Rogue approached her.

Klaya squinted hard and tried to recall. She gasped and opened her eyes. "Wolf."

Chapter Nine

The residual shame of her emotional letdown in front of the guys had clung to her like wet clothing for days. Waking up in a cold sweat and screaming for her life the last few mornings didn't make matters any less dramatic. Klaya had withdrawn and kept to herself. She hated how vulnerable she had become, and despised the fact she didn't mind the guys' unconditional support and attention through it all. For her to be held by the wolves when she tremored held a bitter sweetness she didn't allow herself to overindulge in. The moment she became fully conscious and aware, she scampered off to the water to regain her composure.

Rogue and Seth had been sweet and accommodating. They supported her willingly, and backed off when she was resistant to it. Fending for herself in the woods earlier in the day hadn't let off

83

the tension she had hoped for, in part because her protectors trailed her from a distance, but more so, because the freedom was overcast by the looming danger of the armed assassins returning. Mere days had dragged by but seemed like weeks. The last thing she could handle was the cabin fever, or, as circumstances would have it, cave fever that had set in.

"You know, my...uh...episode, the other day was entirely too serious." Klaya scrubbed her face with her palms then dug through each of the backpacks in quest of something she was sure Gee would have sent. She needed to lighten the mood.

"But necessary. How you holding up, gorgeous?" Rogue shot her a wink from over by the fire. "You've been pretty quiet."

"I know, thanks for respecting my need for time and space. I feel"–she reflected with astonishment— remarkably better."

"I'm glad to hear it." Seth sat beside his brother.

"We've got full bellies. We are safe and protected, surrounded by powerful elements. I think it's time to unwind a little. I'm not a big fan of being uptight and stressed out."

"Given the situation, it's understandable." Seth's

84

sweet smile warmed her heart. Those incredible brown orbs caused a stir deep inside.

Klaya needed more than safety now. She needed to cut loose. Her cougar was clawing to break free. Focused on her task at hand, she searched relentlessly. "Come on, I know it's here." She tossed Rogue's empty bag next to his strewn clothing and moved on to Seth's.

"What are you looking for?" Seth chuckled.

"Gee's got a bar and...." She felt the empty bottom of the pack and threw it aside and started on the duffle bags next. The first one, clothes and towels, the second one, canned goods and provisions. In the last bag, the only one untouched since their arrival, she dug deep and smiled with relief. "I knew he had to have given us something." She tugged out a tall box with a big grin. On top, written in black marker were the words: *When you're feeling a little better, have a few, on me. Gee.* Klaya tore the tape off the edges and tugged out a large bottle of tequila, a container of orange juice, a bottle of grenadine, a small jar of maraschino cherries, and three plastic tumblers. It was perfect for her needs. *I have got to get that bear some jars of honey when this is all over.*

"He sent fruity drinks?" Rogue snickered.

85

"Not exactly, my dear wolf-boy. He sent the makings for my favorite libation. Tequila sunrise." She dug deeper into the box and pulled out a salt shaker and three limes. "Very nice, Gee," she crooned. Klaya leered over at the brothers with mischief in mind. "Care to join me?"

An hour or so and three rounds later, the tequila had somewhat smoothed her shattered nerves. An extraordinary ease rolled over her muscles, and she stretched her neck side to side to release the last of her tension.

"These drinks are kick ass." Rogue grabbed the stemmed cherry from the top of his drink and chomped down on the fruit. "I'm feeling pretty good." The juice left a slight shine on his perfect lips, as though it was beckoning her to taste them.

The remainder of her inhibitions melted away with another sip. The longing she'd tried to hold at bay for days crashed over her like a tidal wave. She considered the wolves sitting across the fire from her. Both handsome, with rugged features of strong jawlines, striking orbs, and powerful arms she was dying to be wrapped in. The scruffy facial hair they had acquired since their arrival added primal appeal. A flash of them stripped down, before they shifted

86

resonated in her memory. Warmth filled the apex between her thighs with anticipation. Fire burned in her bones at the wild thoughts of being sandwiched between the two of them with them kissing, stroking, and penetrating her, and she liked it. Any thoughts of mourning were a distant blur amongst the fever curling around her spine.

Klaya got to her feet and paced the length of the cave, drink clutched in hand as she disputed her own internal ramblings, the mental prattle of physical want and need. The crackle of the blazing wood, the glimmer of the crystals along the walls, and the light of the moon peering through the stone ceiling proved even more intoxicating than the alcohol.

Despite the power of her tequila-induced craze, an element of fear thrummed in her chest, the fear of reaching out, of rejection, but, more so, of reciprocated attraction. After all, she felt the *Nasc*. The jolt in her arms when she lost her balance on the rocks, when they caught her—she received a powerful jolt from both of them. They had told her it happened the first time they touched her, pulling her from inside the tree. To top it all, there was no denying the magnetic pull she felt for them, her draw to them both amplified in strength as they spent time together. The three curled up next to the fire each night, one on either side of her. Even without physical contact, they managed to sheath her in a blanket of security and tenderness.

In her years growing up amongst the Cytaana Clan, she knew of the *instantaneous thunderbolt*, the bond only happens with destined mates. What she had never heard of was the possibility to experience it with any shifter other than a cougar. Now, here she was, face-to-face with two divine specimens of virility and strength, with a searing attraction she couldn't dispel. Desire burned deep, and she couldn't fight it anymore. Being within close proximity heightened the shock wave of yearning. Each glance, smile, and the slightest touch of their hands to hers set every nerve in her body on fire with unquenched desire.

Klaya paused and tried to steady her shaky fingers, mustering the courage she needed most right now. "How's your drink, Seth?" She sat down adjacent to them.

"Fantastic." He grinned.

A surprising playfulness rolled over her. "Bet there's something I can do neither of you can."

"Climb trees, catch wild game, outrun us?" Seth chimed in with a curious smile.

"Oh, those things." She waved off his innocence. "I mean something a little more...sassy."

"Such as?" Rogue narrowed his eyes.

She collected her own garnish and held it up in front of her mouth with a smirk. "Can you tie your cherry stem into a knot, boys?"

"It's not rocket science. Sure." Rogue took the bait and started twisting his between his fingers.

"Anyone can do it like that...I mean, with no hands?"

Rogue and Seth lowered their cups and glanced at each other with wide eyes.

"You can tie it in a knot, with no hands?" Seth's disbelief spurred her on.

She winked and popped the juicy morsel into her mouth. She gripped and tugged with her teeth and devoured the delectable sweetness. "I most certainly can." Klaya winked and tilted her head back. Satisfied with her captive audience, she eased the stem into her mouth. She swirled her tongue over twisting it into a circle and utilized her teeth as she tucked one end through the hole. Content with her performance, she parted her lips and held the knot between her teeth. She collected it between her thumb and fingertip with a grin and presented her prize to her observers. "Ta da."

"Holy shit!" Rogue squirmed and adjusted his pants.

Klaya glanced down, pleased with his unmistakable bulge. She snickered when she caught sight of Seth tucking his shirt over his zipper.

"Your talent is, uh...." Seth's voice was gruff.

"Mind-blowing," Rogue offered in a throaty whisper.

A rush of heat shot through her core. The lust in their gazes was exactly what she'd hoped for, but their stares also held apprehension. She chugged the rest of her drink, determined not to waver. "Anyone care to join me for a dip?" She nodded over to the waterfall. "I'm a little warm right now."

Klaya stood up and unbuttoned her jeans. She inched them down her hips to her feet, and stepped out of them. Vulnerability crept in as they remained still, focus glued on her exposed legs. She eased her shirt over her head and dropped the material on the ground at her side. Clad in only her lace panties and bra, she became irritated with their lack of response.

"Suit yourselves." She spun with a huff and headed for the falls. Klaya unhitched her bra and tossed it aside then slipped her panties off and dove into the water. If this didn't work, perhaps a cold shower would tame the burning desire amplifying in her core. She swam deep under the water, desperate to wash away her longing. She ascended for a gulp of air and dove under again, avoiding the urge to look for the wolves. Klaya headed to the falls and surfaced under the cascading water. Part of her wanted to cry with disappointment, but she held it back.

Despite her pruning fingers after what seemed an eternity in the water, there was no way in hell she was leaving her cascading retreat. Humiliation rippled through her chest. Klaya closed her eyes and let the falling water spill over her head and shoulders with the hopes the tequila would minimize their memories of the sexually depraved cougar, come the morning. Worst case scenario, she could claim drunk and disorderly as the leading cause to save face the next day. For now, hiding out was her only reprieve.

"Is there room for two more?" Seth's velvety voice startled her. Klaya whipped around to find both brothers, shirtless, just feet away from her in the water. Her pulse raced. Butterflies took flight in her stomach.

Klaya hugged herself, covering her exposed breasts, not sure of what their arrival meant. "I didn't think you were interested." Her teeth chattered from the cold.

"Oh." Rogue nodded with arched brows. "We're interested."

"Talk about an understatement," Seth interjected. "We aren't supposed to...." He threw brother a pleading glance.

"Ryker threatened to tear us a new one if we tried anything with you." Rogue's confession brought a flood of relief to her weary soul.

"I see." Still cautious of pending rejection, she treaded carefully. "And now?"

"We aren't sure how to read you, Klaya. With everything you've been through, we didn't want to overstep...." Seth scrubbed his furry chin.

"You aren't. I wouldn't have gotten through any of this without you, either of you. You saved my life," she asserted.

"Anyone would have stopped the hunters—" Seth began.

"The hunters are not what I meant." She inched closer to them. "The way you've been here for me. If I had been alone, I don't know that I wouldn't have given up, or gone on a suicide mission of revenge." Finally, she had a chance to express her gratitude.

"If you had any idea how much restraint we've had to use this week...." Rogue shook his head, torment marring his features.

"Restraint?"

"My God, Klaya, from the moment we first saw you." Seth's sweet demeanor faded, and dark lust filled his eyes. "I've spent more time in this cold shower then I care to admit. The moment you were asleep, we've both had to cool off. We didn't trust ourselves."

"I had no idea." Excitement curled around her spine. "And now?"

"Ryker may snap our necks." Rogue inched closer to her. "A single night with you would be worth it. Your scent drives me over the edge."

"Drives us both. You're the most gorgeous woman we've ever seen." Seth moved closer.

A shiver raced down her spine, and heat spread through her pussy. "You want me? Both of you do?"

"Fuck yes," they recited.

"Then, take me." She lowered her arms in surrender.

The wolves approached and Klaya's heart pummeled with excitement. Their hair dripped and glistened under the moonlight. Their bronzed skin encased perfectly chiseled muscles from their smooth chests all the way down their corrugated abs. Her breathing hitched.

Rogue was the first to make contact. He cupped her face with both hands and drew her close, the heat of his sweet breath brushing over her face. He swooped down and planted a feathery kiss on her lips and then retreated, staring into her eyes with a smile. She raked her fingers through his mass of curly blond hair and pulled him closer for more. He claimed her mouth again, this time with urgency. Klaya's knees buckled as his tongue curled around hers and swept the inside of her mouth. From behind, the delectable heat of Seth's mouth trailed down the length of her neck along her shoulders. He smoothed his hands over her breasts and rolled her hardened nipples between his fingers.

Lost in the passion of Rogue's kiss, a pleasant surprise rubbed against the inside of her thigh, and another against the cheek of her ass. *They weren't only shirtless.* She gasped with delight. Klaya dipped her head back as the brothers devoured her throat and shoulders. They stroked her skin and pressed their bodies tight against hers. The wolf sandwich she had been so famished for was even more tantalizing than she'd imagined. Seth kneaded her left breast with one hand, and slid his other down to her aching pussy. He massaged her throbbing clit with delicious circles; her thighs twitched.

Rogue kissed down the front of her neck and captured her right nipple between his teeth. He licked and whisked her tender peak. Tingles of arousal shot through her core. Klaya gripped the massive length of Rogue's erection and reached her other hand behind her and captured Seth's. Two magnificent cocks, all to herself. She wanted her wolves to bury themselves deep inside her right then and there.

"Klaya, I want to taste you," Seth whispered in her ear. He nibbled her lobe. Tingles of excitement trailed down the length of her spine.

"Don't be greedy, bro. We take turns." Rogue moved up to her mouth and reclaimed.

Klaya eased back from his reach with a grin. "No need to fight. I think we could all use a snack." She stroked their cocks, hungry for her own treat.

"You're shivering." Rogue planted a gentle kiss on her lips and collected her hand. He led the way to the steps and out of the water.

Chapter Ten

The wolves set up blankets for three by the fire. Klaya had another naughty bit of fun in mind. Determined, she grabbed the salt, the limes, and the tequila, and brought it over to the makeshift bed. Her knife in hand, she sliced up the green fruit on a plate and collected their empty glasses then poured generous amounts of liquor and lined them up beside the lime. Her skin, still moist from the pool, had the perfect start to the next drink.

"Anyone interested in another round?" She knelt down on the blanket and arched backward as she sprinkled the salt on her stomach. Klaya placed a wedge of lime between her teeth with a grin.

The brothers each grabbed a glass and knelt in front of her. Rogue slid his tongue up the salted length of her belly then sucked up his shot. He descended on her lips for the first taste of lime, with a sour but decadent kiss. He lingered for an enjoyable moment then retreated. Klaya replaced the lime with a new one and Seth duplicated his round.

"Now for mine." She sprinkled the salt on Seth's chest and licked with a moan of satisfaction. She chugged her drink and stole the lime he still had between his teeth. He responded with a teasing kiss. She repeated the same on Rogue. The heat of tequila trickled down her chest and into her tummy. A warm buzz shot through her body.

The boys collected the cups and put them to the side. Klaya lay down on the blanket and Rogue knelt between her legs. Seth rested on his knees, above her head. No words were spoken; they had a divine rhythm of sexual sync she never realized was possible.

Rogue gripped her knees and eased her legs open. He buried his face between her thighs and she gasped with pleasure. He captured her mound with his heated mouth and gently sucked, much the same way he kissed her mouth. As she trembled with delight, he trailed along her delicate folds and whisked her clit with his talented tongue then slipped a finger inside and gently massaged her inner walls.

Rogue stroked her to heightened bliss.

Seth gripped his swollen cock above her famished lips. She tilted her head back and gripped his shaft, bringing it to her lips. The hardened ridge of his thick head beckoned her, and she licked around the width of it. A deep throaty moan escaped his mouth. Klaya took the tip of his cock into her mouth and cradled it with her tongue. Deeper with each stroke, she inched his hardened flesh in and out, her intention to bring him to the brink of ecstasy. She cupped his balls and massaged with gentle fingers. The farther she took Seth in, the more intensely Rogue worked on her clit.

Jolts shot through her, making it hard to focus on pleasing her second wolf. Determined to outlast them both, she took his cock farther in until it touched her throat; she palmed the base of his shaft and gripped a little tighter. Long, deep pushes in and out of her mouth; she sucked and twirled her tongue around the ridge of his cock.

"Holy fuck, now I get how you tied the cherry stem," he grunted. "You keep doing this, I'm gonna come." He inched away from her. "Not yet," he wheezed. Seth ran his fingers through her hair and caressed her cheek tenderly. He leaned down and captured her lips in a slow, drugging kiss. The intensity grew with each exchange, she panted between kisses, his tongue danced with hers.

Rogue increased the pace of his fingers and mouth, rubbing her clit. Klaya moaned long and deep. She shifted her hips, moving in sync with his suck.

"Oh God," she gasped, body ablaze, the building swells radiated from her core and exploded into divine convulsions.

"Yeah, baby, come for me." Rogue lapped up the wetness as it spilled out of her.

"Looks tasty," Seth hummed.

Rogue stroked her clit to completion and sat up with a grin. His lips glistened with her juices. With a nod, they traded places.

Klaya shivered from residual tremors under Seth's seductive gaze before he dove down for his own taste.

Rogue knelt above her head, and she angled her neck and slipped the tip of his cock into her mouth eagerly. She licked around the ridge of his head and slowly devoured his sinewy flesh. He grunted hard, but didn't push. Klaya paced herself with his length and girth. Both men were very well-endowed, and rock hard. She eased him out of her mouth and slipped her finger over the drop of pre-cum and spread it over the tip with a grin. "Mmm," she hummed, and took the full head into her mouth. The savory liquid spurred her on. She sucked a little harder, and gripped the base of his shaft as she angled herself and accepted his full length into her throat.

She took him deep and long in slow strokes while Seth sucked her clit, bringing her close to the brink for the second time.

"Fuck," Rogue groaned, he inched out of her grasp, "I want inside you, Klaya."

"Oh yes, please," she crooned.

Seth had a talent of his own, with two fingers inside her and a different motion of sucks and swirls. Electric currents of heat surrounded her clit and her pussy tightened. "Oh, yes." She bit her lip as spasms filled her core. Klaya panted as she rode the frenzy of explosions.

"I think she's happy," Seth's deep voice resonated through her body. He licked and sucked her juices.

"I want you both," she gasped. "Right now."

"Any preference who and where?" Rogue

whispered.

"Lie down, you'll both have a turn on each side, if I get my way."

She glanced at Seth, happy to find him nodding. "Your wish is our command."

Rogue did as she asked and Klaya straddled him, resting up on her knees. She leaned down and stole another kiss. Her pulse raced; her core thrummed with pleasure. He gripped her ass and gave it a firm slap, and she gasped with excitement.

"So, you like it rough?" he taunted.

"You'll be amazed with what I like." She caressed his tongue with hers and reached behind her for Seth to come closer.

Rogue's rigid cock rubbed along the inside of her thigh. She gripped his head and glided it through her wet folds. She slipped a finger over her swollen flesh and parted her opening for him. Rogue darted his tongue in and out of her mouth with a tease, the taste of her juice still on his lips. She braced his head against her pussy and trembled with anticipation. Behind her, Seth moved close and grabbed her ass with heated palms. He blazed a trail of kisses along her shoulder and nipped her skin with playful bites.

Klaya eased herself down onto Rogue's rock-hard

cock. She slid down his length with a deep moan of gratification as his thickness filled her. "Oh, fuck," she gasped. She glided up and down his length. Seth pressed his cock against her cheek and cupped her breasts with firm hands. He rolled and twisted her nipples between his fingers while he nibbled on her neck and shoulder. Dripping with moisture, she was ready for more. She collected Seth's right hand and guided it down to her pussy as she took all of Rogue's cock deep inside her.

Seth traced his finger along her slick wetness and spread it over her ass, prepping for double entry. Her breath hitched at his touch, tender but determined. A sharp but joyful sting shocked her when he slipped a moistened finger in her ass. "Oh, yes," she begged. "More...please." He collected more wetness from her pussy and slathered it over his target. He inserted a second finger and worked his way to acclimatize her ass for him.

"I want you both inside me." She gave a winded plea. "Now, Seth, fuck me." He pressed down on her shoulders and angled her over. She was face-to-face with Rogue once again. The position granted him even deeper entry to her pussy.

Rogue's long, sensuous kiss distracted her from

the anticipation of what was to come. Seth sank the head of his cock gently inside and a sweet sting filled her ass. She grunted with delight. "Uh, yes." She reached behind her and clawed at Seth's hip. "Deeper," she begged. With each tender stroke, Seth sunk a little farther inside. "I want all of you," she gasped.

Rogue delivered a long, intoxicating kiss that drew her in. The walls of her pussy began to constrict. "Fuck, you're so tight," he grunted. He gripped her hips and the three rode in perfect unison. Their pace intensified and Seth stroked her clit as he rammed into her ass.

"Oh God, I'm close." she cried out. "So close, harder. It feels so good," she whimpered.

Rogue slammed his pelvis upward with each thrust. Seth pummeled her ass. The harder they fucked, the louder they grunted and groaned. Their voices echoed throughout the cave, tempered by the waterfall in the distance. Her inner cougar roared with delight. "Yes," she growled.

They both thrust hard and deep, over and over, Seth rubbed her clit in frantic circles. Rogue cupped her tits, and consumed her mouth with passionate kisses. Both brothers' breaths grew fast and uneven.

They hammered into her with relentless pounding.

Klaya's pussy tightened; every muscle in her body contracted. "Oh, yes, yes," she screamed out as a dizzying explosion rocked her core and shot out to every nerve ending in her body with fiery eruption.

"I feel you, Klaya," Rogue grunted. He pulled her hard onto him.

"So tight," Seth huffed. "I'm ready."

"Me, too." Rogue narrowed his eyes, but watched hers with determination. "What do you want us to do to you, Klaya?"

She panted.

"Tell us," he commanded.

"Please, come inside me." Her inhales grew ragged.

"Where do you want it?"

"In my pussy." she pleaded.

"What about me, Klaya?" Seth growled.

"In my ass." She rode wave after wave of rapture. "Please, give it to me, now."

"Fuck, I'm coming," Rogue hollered. He slammed upward and held her tight as he stiffened in release and pulsed inside her.

Exquisite pain punctured her shoulder as Seth clamped his teeth onto her flesh. "I'm...uh...uh...." He gave a harsh moan and gripped her hips as he pushed hard into her ass.

They convulsed and writhed together, shuddering in completion. Klaya slowed her pace and rode their pulsating cocks.

Seth kissed the tender spot of her flesh where he had bitten her and ran his heated palms along the length of her back. "Are you okay?" he rasped.

"I'm better than okay." She turned her head to the side. Seth leaned over her shoulder and delivered a tender kiss.

"That was fucking amazing." Rogue cupped her face and brought her close to him for another taste of her lips.

Chapter Eleven

The first to awaken, Klaya kissed Rogue's perfect lips then twisted on her other side and kissed Seth. A delightful night filled with two hot guys and endless climaxes. She grinned from ear to ear. The three lay snuggled up under the blankets by the fire. Not only had she had a variety of three-ways with her wolves, she'd also indulged in a few single romps with each of them. Every moment had been pure fulfillment. Their union was solidified, much to her pleasant surprise.

Energized with satisfaction, she inched out from between the brothers. The inherent need to venture out for a solitary hunt took hold. What could an hour alone hurt? They wouldn't miss her. No doubt she'd worn them out with a full night of nonstop fucking. They had been so wonderful about the hunts and cooking meals for her, the prospect of surprising them with the same held great appeal. Klaya spotted the pile of clothes she had dropped by the fire but left them there. She shifted and bolted out of the cave.

Long and fast, she barreled through the towering trees. The shadows cast by the swaying limbs and the scent of pine and cedar invigorated her. This was the most alive she'd felt since before she was shot. A flash of Griffith rushed through her mind, but she shoved it aside, determined to savor the joy of last night. He would never have faulted her for being among the wolves; he was the one who'd sent her to them. His friendship with Drew had solidified his acceptance of the pack. They had talked about it from time to time over the years as their breed died off. Should anything happen to either of them, they'd made a pact never to give up. To move on because it was what Cytaana do—they survived.

No guilt resided in her heart or her mind for lying with the wolves. The only guilt she possessed was not having the power to save her brother, her last surviving family, from his horrible fate. But he went down fighting, exactly like Gee had said to her. He was right. Griffith wouldn't have had it any other way.

Klaya halted on the spot when a delectable scent

struck her palate. *Venison.* She crouched down and scanned the length of the forest. On the far side, the east where the sun rose stood a small doe. Not nearly as big as the boys had brought her, but she would do nicely for a hearty brunch. On the prowl, she crept ever so slowly to avoid alarming her prey. It chomped on leaves from a small bush. Inch by inch, she approached, silent and stealthy. Klaya licked her lip with anticipation. A cool breeze rushed past her. The doe lifted its head and sniffed the air. She was downwind, and it had caught her scent. It bolted toward the west, and she catapulted in hot pursuit.

The carcass was heavy. She dragged her trophy through the entrance of the cave and down the narrow tunnel. The muscles of her shoulders strained under the weight. Klaya heaved it to the fireside and dropped the beast. She glanced around; the brothers were gone from their bed. Her heart raced. New scents crept up her nose. The hair on her neck prickled with fear. She let out a low growl. Klaya braced herself and shifted. She grabbed her clothes and dressed. A quick visual inventory showed other than their clothes, nothing was missing. The weapons she had left strewn beside the bags remained; she grabbed the shotgun and opened the chamber.

Empty. She tore open the box of ammo and loaded a shell into it.

Shuffles at the foot of the cave echoed in her sensitive ears. She stood and aimed the shotgun down the tunnel. Her chest pounded with fright. One, two, four.... Four sets of footsteps echoed down the tunnel toward her. Another long whiff put her fear at ease. Two of them were familiar. Her wolves had returned. She sniffed hard again and lowered the gun. The other two, she also recognized.

"Where the hell have you been?" Rogue approached with a snarl.

"Excuse me?" She gnashed her teeth. "I'm not a child; don't talk to me like—"

The other men came into sight. A plethora of emotions crashed over her. Stunned, she placed the gun on the ground.

"You had us worried sick." Seth stuck close to Rogue's side, gripping his arm.

"I needed to hunt." The others approached and she fixed her gaze on her long lost friend. "Drew?" Ryker walked next to his alpha. She couldn't move. Residual grief surged through her chest again with the appearance of her friend.

"Klaya." Drew crossed over to her and stared at

her, sorrow filled his eyes. "I'm so sorry about Griffith. I can't believe he's gone."

Tears spilled down her cheeks. For the first time since Griffith was murdered, she felt like she was home. "I've missed you so much."

"It's okay, you're here now, we'll figure out what to do." He patted her shoulder.

"When did you get here?" She stared at Drew with disbelief. It had been years since she had seen him. He was a far cry from the young, angry lad she'd met in the bar. Drew had filled out and carried a powerful stance, with a calm demeanor. Alpha suited him well.

"We arrived past the ridge, but these two were out searching for you." He chuckled. "I told Gee these numskulls couldn't keep you locked up."

Klaya snickered with amusement through tears. She ran the back of her hand across her cheeks and wiped away the moisture. He had developed a knack for shifting the mood with his dry humor.

***

"This is some good food." Drew grinned as he chomped down on the roasted meat.

"Klaya's favorite," Seth chimed in.

"I remember. You were never much for rabbit," he concurred.

The five sat around the fire over lunch.

"When we woke up, you were gone, had us half scared to death," Rogue snarled, anger dulling his striking green eyes.

"I'm sorry." She avoided his stare. Seth was less hostile and offered a tender smile.

"I could have warned you, Klaya was never one to stay put if there was deer nearby," Drew recalled with a tone of amusement.

"How much longer do we have to stay here?" The last of her joy had dissipated under Rogue's continual scowl. The dire need to flee and be free of them coursed through her veins.

Ryker spoke for the first time since their arrival. "Pack trackers caught the scent of a few humans right outside of our territory, but there has been no attempt to enter Los Lobos."

"Does that mean they're gone?" Hope rose for a moment.

"I don't think so." The enforcer pursed his lips.

"Klaya." Drew leaned forward. "I know this is pretty raw for you, but when the guys filled me in on everything...." He looked over to the brothers.

Panic set in. "Everything?"

Seth shook his head. "What you told us about the day you got shot, where you were, the men, the smells. We brought him up to speed so you wouldn't have to go over it all, again."

"Oh." She nodded with relief. "Thank you."

Drew shifted sideways and faced her. "You described something that sounded all too familiar to me."

"I did?"

"Remember when you and Griffith saved one of our wolves?"

"Like it was yesterday."

"The guys who tortured him caught him days before you guys found him. They had him locked up, in a cellar, strung up by chains, from what he told us. When they brought him out to the forest, they were trying to release and track him down."

"I hadn't realized. He didn't talk much while he was with us." She slumped her shoulders.

"Your experience bears a remarkable similarity to what he told us. So much, I can't overlook it." He let out a quiet growl. "Not when it cost Griffith his life, and nearly cost you yours."

White-hot shock zapped through her stomach. "You think the people who hurt your wolf were connected to the hunters who killed my brother?"

"I do." He glanced to her with narrowed eyes and flexed the muscles of his jaw.

"There's more, isn't there?" She dipped her chin down, fatigue washing over every muscle in her body.

Drew didn't speak right away. "Gee has a theory. I don't think you'll like it, but you need to hear it."

Klaya cupped her hands behind her neck to fend off the muscle spasm building with every word. She readied herself for impact. She suspected he was about to reveal the very speculation she had toyed with since the fateful morning they were attacked. "Let me guess." She stared up at the sunlight through the ceiling. "He thinks maybe these guys weren't merely diehards out to get their rocks off. His theory has to do with the disappearance of the Cytaana clan and why there may be none left?"

"Yeah, but a few wolves have gone missing over the years, too. Then, the murders in Keystone." Drew glanced over to the brothers. "We still have no clue why or by whom."

"You think it's all connected?" She cocked her head.

113

Seth cleared his throat. "When you told us about that day, you said you *smelled death in the cellar.* Distinctive scents?"

"Other cougars," she recalled aloud, and then it hit her. "Oh my God, and wolves."

Ryker put his plate down and stared at Drew with raised brows. Drew nodded and Ryker spoke. "Klaya, Doc pulled a high-tech tracking device out of your arm."

"Yes?"

"They all wore combat gear, had military-grade riffles and ammo, we figure this is an organized group, hunting shifters and eliminating them."

"Why?" She couldn't fathom the notion, yet couldn't dispute the logic.

"I need to know how they found you and Griffith."

"I don't know?" She shook her head with despair.

Drew interjected. "Okay, let's take this one step at a time. What happened before the attack?"

Klaya's chin quivered. To recount the events again was more than she could bear. She swallowed hard. "We were going to sleep; it was first light of day."

"What happened before?" Rogue spoke with a

softer voice than earlier, one suggesting empathy rather than irritation.

"We came home from an all-night hunt." The words rolled off her tongue and resonated in her brain, and her breath caught in her throat. "They spotted us in the forest." Revelation stung her heart. "They must have tracked us back to the cabin. We were going to sleep. Oh God." She pulled her knees to her chest and rocked back and forth. "It's my fault." She clasped her hand over her mouth with horror. "I wanted to hunt deer. He said it was too risky. I told him he was being overprotective." Klaya fixed her stare on her plate of half-eaten food beside her and snatched it up in a rage. She slammed it into the fire and screamed, "It was my fault."

Rogue grabbed her by the shoulders and lifted her to her feet. He gathered her into his arms. "It's not your fault, don't ever think that."

"If there's one thing I knew about my buddy, no one ever made him do what he didn't want to. Not even his kid sister, sweetheart. Think about it." The quiet reflection in Drew's tone held truth. "Anytime he dug his heels in, there was no way to change his mind."

Even with endless hours of torture, the assassins

couldn't force him to shift for them. Still, her mind raced. She'd goaded Griffith to go for the night hunt, and dismissed his cautionary resistance as his typical role of the overbearing big brother.

"We need to know where you were, Klaya. I know it's hard, but before Seth and Rogue found you on the edge of Black Hills, do you remember anything about where you were?" Drew pried carefully.

The comfort of Rogue's arms grew restrictive with Drew's continued interrogation. She placed her palms on the younger wolf's chest then eased to stand on her own two feet. Klaya wiped the tears off her cheeks and mustered her strength to focus on the task at hand. "Our cabin was out on the east side of Keystone. They hit me with something there, and I woke up in the cellar. I don't know how long I was out." She stepped to the side, desperate for some physical space, the weight of the world resting on her aching shoulders now.

"When you awoke, Griffith bought you some time and you managed to escape?" Drew persisted.

Klaya searched her weary brain for something, any minute detail she could recall. "The forest was like this, cedar and pine, lots of birch, too. It was all forest. There was only enough clearing for the cabin."

"It was a cabin?" Ryker stood.

The faint details grew clearer. "Yes, an old board and batten, faded wood, untreated, had a gray tone to it. The stairs led out from a storm cellar, the doors flapped open." She fought the blur to remember more. "The smells...gas. There were trucks and vans, maybe four or five, newer vehicles. Something was burning."

"Wood?" Seth rose as well.

"No." She pondered the odor. "Propane." She snapped her head up.

"Like a barbeque?" Drew stepped closer.

"More like a furnace. It was a single-story dwelling, but a fair size."

Ryker turned to Drew. "We can narrow it further."

"It's a stretch, but it's more than we had this morning." He nodded. "Klaya, before they shot you, how long do you think you were running?"

"Maybe a few miles, not long at all. I broke through the forest, past a small clearing. There was a creek, and then I headed into more forest. Then the bullet, and the rest is blank."

"Ryker, you have the map here?"

"Yes." Ryker headed over to his backpack

117

propped against the cave wall.

"A small clearing, a creek, not far from the Black Hills boundary. That gives us a good location to search and narrow down the cabins in the area." Drew nodded at her. "Thank you, Klaya."

Rogue approached her again. He took her into his arms and kissed her forehead. "You did awesome, babe."

Seth cupped her cheek. "Yeah, fantastic."

Chapter Twelve

Rogue held Klaya tight. The invisible weight of worry lifted from his chest. He found relief she was able to make some headway with the information. Her pain proved a tangible wound to him. He wanted to do nothing more than eradicate it and anything causing her pain. The aggression it provoked toward his alpha and the enforcer wasn't acceptable. He understood it and yet, when Ryker settled his gaze on them, silent judgment seeming to fill his black eyes, Rogue could barely suppress a growl. Intellect warred with instinct.

"She was off-limits."

"We can explain." Seth held his hands up in surrender. His brother would rather joke and cajole, fighting only when necessary

Instincts winning, Rogue kept her under one arm and faced Ryker with a defiant glare. "Get away from her." It didn't matter how far away the enforcer stood, Rogue would defend her.

"What?" Cool challenge underscored Ryker's single syllable.

"It's not their fault," Klaya hissed. When she would have stepped in front of him, he and Seth moved as one to bracket her. Their protective grasps on her were met with lightning bolts of electricity jolting from her skin to Rogue's. Visible sparks flew from where he and Seth's hands touched her.

Drew stepped forward. "Stop. Everyone."

Seth and Rogue stood in guard of Klaya, and Ryker remained still, with his infamous stone-cold expression.

"Klaya." Drew faced her. "Did I see what I think I did?"

"All this testosterone is making me sick." She pulled away from everyone and circled the fire. Icy emptiness encased Rogue's heart at her resistance to his protection.

"Klaya, talk to me," Drew commanded.

"It was...it is. *The Nasc*," she confessed.

"Oh shit." Drew scrubbed his face with his palms. "You and Griffith told me about it, but said neither of you ever experienced it. You're sure?"

"Without a doubt, it's the third time since we've met."

"With both of them?"

"Both," she concurred.

"What the hell are you talking about?" Rogue grumbled. Had she lost her mind?

Seth squinted with confusion. "Yeah, what is going on?" He crossed his arms and pressed his lips tight. An uncharacteristic stance for his passive little brother, in Rogue's opinion.

Angst tore at Rogue's stomach. He watched how Klaya stared at Drew and shrugged but said nothing. Her feisty stance softened and she dropped her hands to her sides, seeming helpless to offer an explanation.

The hardened stare Drew shot toward Rogue and his little brother settled in his gut like lead. Drew forced a huge sigh through pursed lips. "Klaya's shifter species has a different—bond than wolves."

Rogue exhaled a frustrated breath. "Klaya?"

She bit her bottom lip and hesitated.

"Talk," Rogue growled.

"Fine," she snapped. "In the Cytaana clan, when destined mates connect, physically, especially when there's a protective need present, there is an exchange of energy." She glanced over to Drew. "The thunderbolt bond or *the Nasc* is the way Cytaana discover who their destined mates are."

"This shock we just felt?" Seth cocked his head.

"Yes, you said you felt it when you pulled me from the tree?"

"Both of us did," Rogue agreed.

"And again, when you caught me on the rocks and stopped me from falling?"

"Right." Seth nodded.

"And, this time, I was the protective one because I was afraid Ryker would hurt you both. It's the mating bond." Embarrassment flooded her and her cheeks grew warm. "That's why—"

"Last night." Rogue grinned.

"Last night," she whispered and gave both her wolves with an affectionate gaze.

"Last night?" Ryker stared at them.

"We didn't try anything," Seth protested.

"That's it," Klaya murmured. She waltzed up to Ryker with her chin lifted. "Look, if you want to blame anyone, it's all on me. I was the aggressor. They were perfect gentlemen the entire time. They protected me, they fed me, and they comforted me through the hardest moments I've ever known in my entire life." She shot a fleeting glance over to Rogue with a smile then turned back to Ryker with a challenging glare. "I. Attacked. Them," she announced with pride. "And, if you have a problem with it, then you discuss it with me, because it won't be the last time."

Rogue's heart pounded. *This woman has guts. No one challenges the pack enforcer. She may not be a wolf, but she's got the same kind of fight in her.* He didn't think it was possible to want her any more than he already did. She proved him wrong. He glanced over to his brother to find Seth covering his half-grin with his hand.

"Cat. Go to your mates." Dismissal rang from the enforcer's statement.

Drew shook his head. Their alpha always seemed to possess immeasurable patience, but even he had his limits. "Yes, Klaya, go to your mates and leave Ryker alone. Friendship only goes so far."

"Okay, now we're all clear on where Klaya stands with"—the alpha glanced over to Rogue and Seth then shook his head—"everything, we need to get down to business."

Seth cleared his throat with a muffled laugh. "Uh, what's the plan?"

"Ryker and I will go over the map and see if we

can't pinpoint an estimated location. Show us where you found her and we can figure it out from there. As it stands, we have no cellular signal up here, so we have to head back to Los Lobos where we can check with some of the guys who deliver propane in the area. Let's see if we can't find our friends before they find Klaya."

"Are we leaving now?" Rogue's heart sank. He scanned the cave. A part of him wanted to stay with her. "We can't put her out in the open."

"We all go," Ryker affirmed. "Together."

"You told me, Rogue," Drew said, his voice was low but stern. "The hunters showed up sniffing around right after you arrived?"

"Yeah, two men did, and they were communicating on radios with others."

"It's only a matter of time before they return. You'll all be sitting ducks now," the alpha asserted. "Pack your gear. We leave within the hour."

Chapter Thirteen

The hike to town was dreadfully quiet. The sun burned bright, the air warmer than it had been on their trek up to the cave. They hiked along the stony ridge. The alpha and enforcer led the way. Klaya followed, and the brothers walked a few feet behind. The bags weren't as heavy since they had two extra bodies to carry the load and threesome had used most of the food they brought and...the tequila. Klaya brushed her lips with the pads of her fingers at the delicious recollection of their late night adventures.

"How ya doin', beautiful?" Rogue's voice was gruff.

"Fine." She glanced over her shoulder with a smile, but her chest tightened with the lie. "Actually, I'm worried."

"About what?" He and Seth caught up to her.

The collective warmth of the wolves surrounding her didn't bring the ease she had hoped for. The muscles of her shoulders tightened with the encroaching worry festering in her stomach for their safety and the risk they accepted in protecting her.

"It's bad enough I got Griffith killed and put you two at risk. Now, we're marching to Los Lobos. What if they come looking for me? People are gonna get hurt, maybe even killed."

Drew shook his head. "Klaya, they've already been here searching for you. Because of the tracer Doc took out at the ranger station, it made sense to have you guys hide up here in case they tried to come to town next to find you. But they showed up here instead. You're a sitting duck up in the cave. It's only a matter of time before they find you there. Back in town, the pack is ready to fight. We have more strength in numbers." He smoothed his hand over her hair.

The words rolling off his tongue didn't sit right with her. "I don't want anyone else hurt or killed because of me." The need to dig her heels in swelled.

"Babe." Rogue cupped her chin. "In case you've forgotten, they've been at this for years. If Gee and Drew are right, they've taken out cougars and wolves alike. The only difference between us protecting you up there"—he motioned to the mountain—"or down there"—he pointed to town—"is we have backup. Believe me, the pack wants payback as much as you do." Rogue removed his hand.

Seth's eyes darkened. "Darlin', we haven't discussed this. But given the new information, I'll bet my life those fuckers are the ones who killed our parents."

Klaya's pulse raced. She glanced to Rogue to find he mirrored his brother's expression. "They tortured your dad?"

Drew folded his arms and nodded. "I didn't tell Rogue and Seth everything."

"What do you mean?" She arched her brows.

"The wolf you and Griffith saved a few years ago?"

"Yeah?"

"He was their dad, Thomas. He was one of our pack." Drew made eye contact with Ryker who gave a nod.

"When Thomas and Sue were killed last year," Drew continued, "they were living outside of Keystone, past the pack territory. My guess is they tracked him down to finish the job you interrupted."

"I didn't know his name." Klaya studied the tapered eyes and gritting teeth of her two wolves. Rage radiated from their bodies. Both brothers dropped their hands to their sides, gripped in fists so tight their knuckles whitened.

Drew flexed his jaw muscles. "He never talked while he was in your care, but when you brought him to town, he told Gee everything."

"Why the hell did we not know about this?" Rogue spewed with a venomous glare toward his alpha.

"Your parents wanted to keep your dad's capture from you because they feared you would try to retaliate."

"You're damn right we would have." Seth crossed his arms over his chest. His breathing sped up and his cheeks grew a dark shade of red.

Klaya looked to Rogue to find him mirroring the exact stance with his broad shoulders squared.

"Thomas had even less information about his capture or the sick bastards who tortured him than Klaya did," Drew continued. "At the time, it seemed random. No one had heard of anything else like this in the area. Because she and Griffith killed them all, it didn't seem likely there were any others."

"He was a wolf." Klaya nodded.

"They both were," Seth concurred.

"The hunters brutalize shifters."

"Yes," Ryker agreed.

"We're only a few miles away now. We need to go, now." Drew swung the duffle bag over his shoulder. "I don't like how exposed we are out in the open."

They headed down the ridge. The hairs on the back of Klaya's neck prickled. She stopped and scanned the nearby tree line. The lack of movement spiked her adrenaline. "We're not alone." She spoke in a hushed voice, loud enough for the guys to all hear her. Ahead of her, Drew and Ryker stopped.

"Klaya, if we get separated, you run for the trees, climb like you did before. Don't stay on the ground." Rogue spoke slow and deliberate in her ear.

"I'm not leaving you, either of you." She glanced behind her.

Thunderous cracks boomed through the air; bullets pinged along the ground and off the rocks all around them. Klaya crouched down and scanned the forest. She spotted six gunmen with rifles behind the first row of trunks.

Ryker shifted into a red wolf with bright amber

eyes. Drew knelt down and growled. His shift took longer, his facial features contorted with agony as he morphed into a magnificent black wolf. When he was done, he nodded to Ryker and they bolted down the ridge and rounded the edge of the forest.

"Stay still," Rogue growled and dropped to his hands and knees. His transformation was instantaneous and he crouched in front of Klaya. Seth shifted next and stood at his brother's flank, they shielded her as bullets zinged by. One assassin dropped to the ground with a murderous roar. Klaya caught a brief glance of the red wolf tearing at his throat and then bolted to the next tree. Two more collapsed, their guns firing off rounds as they crashed to the ground. Wood splintered and scattered in the air. A fourth guy dropped. Seth snarled and blocked her view. To the left, she caught a glimpse of a fifth man collapse. More barrels appeared from beside the trees and the shower of bullets amplified.

A fierce howl in front of her was followed by Seth dropping to the ground.

"Seth?" She crawled over his body to find his shoulder oozing blood. "No!"

Rogue nudged her with his nose and growled. He nodded down the path.

"No, I won't leave either of you here," she barked.

The insistent mate nudged her harder and nipped her in the arm.

"No," she snarled and clutched Seth's bloodied fur.

Seth panted and looked back at her. He nipped at her fingers and bared his teeth. She understood. They wanted to protect her. "Don't make me, please," she sobbed.

Seth got to his feet and curled his lip with another cautioning growl.

"Okay." Klaya bolted down the ridge. The frenzy of fire followed her and she increased her speed. Up ahead, there was a break in the ridge and the forest.

She froze with terror. Rogue caught up to her.

"It's a trap." She crouched down.

Her wolf huddled close to her.

"They're not trying to hit us anymore; they're driving us out into the open." She pointed ahead. "Remember, they don't kill shifters first, they torture. If we go into the clearing, they'll hit us with tranquilizer darts and we're done for."

Klaya glanced around. "The ridge?" She spied over the side. "It's a fifty-foot drop. There's no way without ropes." Frantic she searched around for another escape. More shots rang out. At her side, Rogue let out a blood-curdling yelp and stumbled. Klaya whipped around to find his blond fur seeping crimson as he wobbled backward and fell over the ridge.

No, Rogue! Her heart shattered.

Klaya's stomach bottomed out and jolts of white terror shot through her limbs. Both her wolves were shot. Rogue was dead because of her. A gust of wind rushed past her. The potent waft of gun oil and tobacco stung her nose. The bastard was close. Her lust for blood amplified. There was no way she could protect herself or her wolves in human form. Rage coursed through her veins. The spike of her claws speared through her fingertips, and she roared out in agony as she dropped on all fours as and shifted into her cougar.

There, at the edge of the trees, stood her intended target in camouflage gear. The man who had tormented her and killed her brother. She headed straight for him, fixated on his exposed jugular. A sharp jolt shot through her front leg, and she toppled over and collapsed. Searing pain shot up from her paw to her shoulder. She tried to get up but fell down again. Klaya looked down to her leg to find a bear trap encased her entire foot.

"There's my little bitch. I've been looking for you." He approached with his rifle aimed at her head.

An ear-piercing explosion rocked the very ground she lay on. Dirt and chunks of grass shot up into the air and scattered all around them. Her tormentor dropped to his knees and aimed toward the wolves. "Looks like the cavalry has arrived for your friends," he sneered. "No worries, kitty cat. I've got you for now. That'll do." He removed a gnarled nylon backpack from his shoulder and tugged out a crumpled black net then pulled a small gun from the holster on his thigh, aimed it at her, and pulled the trigger. A sharp sting swept through her neck and everything faded to black.

Chapter Fourteen

B ack in Doc's office at Los Lobos, Seth scowled at the time it was taking. They should be going after the bastards who took Klaya right now. He didn't care about the bullet wound. He had to get her back, at any cost, before it was too late. He growled, seated on the paper-covered table. The pain speared through his shoulder and down his arm. "What the hell are we waiting for?"

If only the physical pain was the real cause of the fire burning through his veins right now. She was hurt and with the hunters. It would be a matter of time before they butchered her like her brother or maybe even worse. He gnashed his teeth at the mere thought of those bastards laying even a finger on his mate.

"Almost got it, buddy. Hang on." Bastian dug the

134

metal prongs deep into his flesh. "There it is." He gripped the tool hard, pulled out the slug, and dropped it into the metal pan on the tray beside him. "You're lucky, no major veins or arteries. It should heal fast without any permanent damage." The pack doctor patched him up.

"I want those sons of bitches." He seethed. "We can't just leave her there." He fired a demanding glare at his alpha who was seated in the chair near the door.

"I talked to Justin. He helped us pinpoint the location of the cabin, and it's one of his delivery sites and no more than three miles outside of pack territory."

"Then, let's go!" Seth hopped off the table.

"Stop." Ryker blocked the doorway with folded arms and a stern glare. "We have a plan."

Seth scrubbed his face with his good hand and snarled. "What is it?"

"First"—Drew got up from the chair and joined Ryker at the door—"we make sure we have everything in place."

"She's out of time. Did you see what happened to her? If she doesn't bleed to death, God knows what the fuck they're doing to her right now."

"Chill, bro," a raspy voice called out from the bed in the corner.

"You're awake?" Seth raced over to his brother.

"Dude, stop with the loud voice. I've got a bitch of a headache." Rogue sat up and clutched his scalp and winced.

"What you have is a mild concussion, five stitches in the back of your skull, and a bullet wound in your side." Doc lifted Rogue's left eyelid and shone a small light as he investigated. "I didn't expect you would wake up for a day or so."

"I'm with Seth. We can't leave her there." He swung his legs over the edge of the gurney.

"While you hot shots have been getting stitched up, we sent Z and Allana to scout the camp and do some recon. They're due back within the hour. We'll meet at Gee's and go over the plan of attack." Drew nodded to the brothers. "Get yourselves to Gee so we can go over what we're doing." He held their stares, the power of the alpha moving through their veins. "She's family to me."

The next hour dragged on for what seemed an eternity to Seth. They sat at the end of bar and sipped on soda water. There was no way they would risk losing their edge.

Gee patted Seth on his good shoulder. "How you holding up, son?"

He grimaced. "Not so good."

"She's a fighter; she'll hang on until we get there." He leaned over to Rogue. "And you, I always said your head was hard as nails, you tough little shit." He nudged his shoulder.

"I guess you're right." Rogue snickered then gripped his head and winced. "Hurts like hell, though."

"What do you expect, when you jump over a fifty-foot ledge?" Drew placed his water on the table and sat down. Ryker stood behind him.

"I wouldn't say jumped." He shrugged. "Shot, stumbled, fell? But definitely didn't jump."

"Good thing you hung on." Ryker nodded.

"Barely." He exhaled. "Thanks for pulling me up."

The enforcer let a faint, uncharacteristic smile slip.

Seth watched the unusual exchange between Ryker and his brother. How odd, that Rogue was able to solicit friendly banter from the stone-cold enforcer, and now, when they should be saving her? Seth had always been the compliant beta. Rogue, marched to the beat of his own drum. At least, it was true until the moment Klaya appeared in their sites. His brother was somehow almost humbled, and Seth had developed a deep-seated need to challenge and take charge. Both their unusual behaviors revolved around her. Their mate, and they needed to move now and make sure they didn't lose her.

"And, I'm sorry for earlier, in the cave." Rogue dipped his chin.

"It's forgotten." Ryker waved off the apology then leaned forward with a stern glare and raised one brow. "But don't let it happen again."

"Never."

Z and Allana strode in from the door and joined them. Allana splayed a map with marks written in red ink across the table. "We spotted eleven guys, three trucks, two vans, and a fully loaded Humvee while we were there. The forest had a few traps set, but no scanners we could find. We can get in undetected, if we're careful."

Z tapped his finger on the paper as he explained. "They have her in the basement; the cellar door is bolted from the outside. Three armed men are with her, four upstairs, and one stationed at each of these lookouts around the cabin. Every person is armed with assault rifles, tranquilizer guns, bulletproof vests, and shoulder-mounted radios. It's a secure line we can't tap into."

Gee plopped into the chair next to Seth. "We don't need huge numbers. We have to move fast, catch them with their pants down, and take them out."

Ryker scraped the stubble of his chin in deliberation. "We need to put those vehicles out of commission."

"I can do it." Allana held up her hunting knife. "I'll slice the tires and disable batteries and weapons." She winked at Seth.

"Let's try to keep the noise down when we get there. If the guys inside get wind of our arrival, it won't be good for Klaya," Drew asserted.

Seth's stomach tensed at the thought of her being harmed any further.

"Z, are you good to hit the scouts in the tree stands?"

"Yup." He nodded.

"Ryker, I want you to crash the main floor, fast assault, and wipe out the four upstairs."

"Done."

"Gee, you and I will storm the basement. We

smoke the three down there and pull her out."

Gee nodded.

Seth glanced around the table. Irritation festered deep inside. "What about us?"

"Yeah?" Rogue echoed.

"You two stay," Ryker said coolly.

"You can't expect us to sit here and do nothing?"

Drew held his hand up and the group went silent. "Guys, I understand. You're pretty banged up. We'll do the heavy work, if you can make the trek, and you'll be there to help her once she's free."

It was better than being glued to a barstool, although bitterness resonated at their limited roles. Seth crossed his arms. "Deal."

Chapter Fifteen

A foul stench filled her nose. Klaya's groggy head pounded. Her eyelids heavy as stone, she forced them open and shook her head to dispel the rancid odor.

"There she is." Her tormentor waved a broken white tube in front of her face. "Smelling salts." He smirked. "Can't have you sleep through everything. It takes half the fun out of it."

Her arms ached over her head, and cold wetness trickled down her left forearm. She was strung up in chains and buck naked. The last thing she remembered was shifting...and the trap. She twisted her left wrist. Pain spiked through her arm at the slightest movement. She glanced up to find her torn flesh dangling from her wrist and blood seeping down her arm.

"What the hell do you want from me?"

141

"Your pain," he hissed.

"What have I ever done to you?" A deadly chill encased her exposed flesh. Her hands were numb.

"Nothing." He shook his head and laughed. "You're simply an abomination and I'm taking you to church, little lady."

Klaya watched him with disgust. He stepped closer to her face and she recoiled. "Abomination?"

"Your kind—half human, half animal—it was not what the good lord intended." He skulked around her with a sadistic smile.

"If that is true, then how the hell do you explain an entire line of shifters who have lasted more than a millennia, you racist piece of shit?"

"Entertainment, of course." He circled her again and trailed a finger along her shoulder. "Your kind has made for great hunting."

"Get your filthy paws off me. I'm warning you," she growled.

He grabbed a fist full of her hair by the base of her skull and yanked her head back hard. The rancid odor of his breath so close to her mouth, she tasted garlic and dental decay against her sensitive palate. Her stomach turned.

"Your friend, the feisty one, he cost me some

good men before you escaped."

"He was my brother, and you cost us our entire race." She seethed.

"Almost. There are still a handful we've been tracking for a few years. Don't worry, they'll join you on the great hunting plain soon enough."

Her pulse raced. "Cytaana? There are more of us?"

"Not for long. But I'm pretty sure you're the last around here, so I'm gonna make this count." He released her hair and waltzed over to a long wooden table where he grabbed a rolled-up leather satchel.

"What is that?" The hairs on her neck barbed.

"Your salvation and my reward." He sprawled it across the table and revealed an arsenal of metal tools.

A painful recollection seared through her brain at the sight of the exact tools he'd forced her to watch him use on Griffith. It was probably the same thing he did to her wolves' father, Thomas. Her belly churned with fire. The urge to shift took hold, but she fought the primal instinct. Griffith wouldn't shift; she wouldn't give him the satisfaction either, not unless she had a shot at tearing this monster apart. No matter what, she wouldn't go down without a fight.

She prayed for the chance to gouge out his eyeballs and tear open his neck first.

Klaya scouted the width of the room. There was dry blood splatter over the concrete walls, a dirt floor, and across the way, the steps which led to freedom. She eyed the doors as her mind raced.

"Don't even think about it. We bolted the door from the outside after your last visit. You won't leave here again...ever." He cackled. Bone-chilling shivers snaked down her spine.

She pondered the details of the room in silence. In a desperate search for any item she could utilize, she scanned the rest of the dungeon. Two armed men stood by the door. The foul stench of tobacco and gun oil filled her palate again.

Klaya smacked her lips with distaste. "Let me guess," she scoffed at them. "You, the hideous one on the left with a scar, I'll bet you're Tin Man." She remembered him lurking below the tree she hid in with Rogue.

"I'm flattered." He smirked.

"You're an asshole," she murmured.

Rogue? The brutal image of him shot over the ridge and of Seth's bloodied shoulder sent daggers of sorrow through her chest. "I'm gonna kill every last one of you pricks." She gritted her teeth.

"That would be quite a feat, given your not-so-distant fate, my feline foe."

The self-righteous murderer selected a tool and returned to her with a long, spiraled tip that eerily resembled a corkscrew. He brushed it across her cheek and down her chest. "Such a pretty little vixen. Wanna screw?" He chortled.

"Go fuck yourself." She spat in his face.

"I've always wondered...." Inquisition filled his shit-brown eyes. "Do you bleed like human women?"

"Have you seen my wrist, you sick son of a bitch?"

"I know you bleed, I take pride in that." He sniggered. "What I mean is, an abomination like you, do you bleed...." He trailed the ice-cold tip of the tool down the length of her belly below her navel.

Klaya fought back her tears of hatred and panic threatening to spill from her eyes.

"Steve," Tin Man called from by the door.

"Can't you see I'm busy here?" He sneered over at him.

"If she's the last one around this place, can't we have a little fun first, before you finish with her?" The thug gripped the crotch of his pants and licked his lips. He elbowed the guy beside him who nodded in agreement.

"You said my name, in front of her." The slime bag spun around as he fumed.

"She's dead soon anyway, what does it matter. Come on, she's naked, and sexy as hell. I want me some real pussy." He chortled.

Steve turned to face her with a leer. He caressed her cheek and she flinched away from his touch. "I suppose this is one area I've neglected to study before." He rubbed the front of his pants, his eyes dilated with grotesque lust.

Bile rose to the top of her throat at the very thought of them near her body. "I'd rather be tortured, kill me now."

"It's a given, my dear, but since you failed to answer my question, about"—he ran his dirty hands down her belly—"whether or not you bleed. I shall have to examine it for myself."

If this was how it would end, Klaya wouldn't allow it, not for a second. It was time to let her cougar out. She waited until the two men put their weapons down. The malignant parasite placed his tool on the table and they surrounded her. This was it. Through the jarring pain of her wrist, she forced the change.

Her claws exploded from her finger tips and her teeth protruded into fangs. She shifted and dropped from the confines of her chains.

The men hollered and scrambled away from her. She pounced on her barbaric captor and slammed him to the ground. In one swift movement, she sank her teeth into his neck and ripped it wide open. The savory taste of copper splattered into her mouth and his blood sprayed over his face. Gurgled gasps slipped through his bloodied lips, he convulsed and gripped his gapping flesh. Clicks of guns cocking snagged her attention from the sheer thrill of revenge. She was prepared to die, but not without a fight. She prowled forward and launched from her hind legs toward the two men by the stairs. Tin Man fired a round and the bullet speared into her chest. She yelped in agony and dropped to the ground. Panting for air, she tried to move, but the stun spread out to her limbs.

As they raised their barrels and aimed at her head, an ear-splitting blast crashed through the doors above them. Splintered wood and chunks of debris collapsed down over the tops of their heads.

"She's here." Drew hopped over the strewn bodies. He crouched down and surveyed the room.

"Shit, she's been shot. Gee, gimme a hand."

Gee barreled into the cellar and helped Drew pick her up. Gee then shoved the bodies off the stairs and cleared the debris. Drew carried her up the steps. The sunlight blinded her momentarily. Klaya sniffed the air, thankful to be free from the stench of death.

"Klaya?" Seth's voice rang out.

Drew set her down on the ground. "She's badly hurt."

"What about...?" Seth stood over her and glanced over to the cellar.

"They're dead." Gee patted his shoulder. "I'm gonna check on Z and the others."

"Klaya, darlin', can you shift for me? Please?" Seth dropped to his knees at her side.

Despite the weakness enveloping her muscles, she triggered the change and shifted back to human form.

Seth inspected her wound. "It's deep. She's bleeding out."

He yanked his T-shirt over his head and tore it into strips. He pressed down on her chest, and Drew lifted her shoulders and fastened the material around her. Her chest throbbed with agony.

Drew whipped off his coat and draped it over her

trembling body. "We have to get you to Doc."

"Are they all dead?" She twisted her head and scanned around them.

Drew called out, "Gee?"

"It's all good here; Ryker got the last of them," he hollered out.

"All dead." Drew nodded.

Ryker rounded the corner with Gee and a woman she didn't recognize.

"I took care of most of the vehicles, but saved the van." The woman approached Drew and glanced down at Klaya. "By the looks of her, we'll need the wheels."

"Yeah, good thinking. Let's get her to the van." Seth lifted her.

Every movement shot jolts of pain through her upper body. "Hold on." She winced. "Let me stand up."

"No," Seth growled.

"Help. Me. Up." She gnashed her teeth.

Seth helped her to her feet then held the coat so she could slip into it and zipped it up.

"Can you walk?" He spoke in a softer tone.

"There's something I have to do." She hobbled along the side of the cabin and rounded the corner.

149

"Where the hell are you going?" Seth followed.

Fueled by adrenaline, she pushed on. "Anyone got a lighter?" She stopped at the long white tank and rested her palm on the cold metal.

The woman approached. "I suppose you want this place lit up?"

With a smile of satisfaction, she nodded. "Obliterated." Klaya's knees buckled and she slumped. Seth caught her and scooped her up into his arms.

Drew barked orders. "Seth, get her into the van. Ryker, round everyone up. Allana, we need a head start."

"You got it."

"Only if I get to watch it blow," Klaya wheezed, her strength drained with every labored breath.

"Go."

Through the rush of chaos, they loaded her in the van. Numbness crept over her body.

Drew climbed inside the van and slammed the door behind him. "Do we have everyone?" he called to the front.

"One more. He's a little slowed down. I'm gonna pick him up," Gee called out with a chuckle.

"Go, she's lost a lot of blood. We don't have much

time."

"Darlin'." Seth knelt on the floor beside her. He took her hand and kissed the inside of her wrist.

Tires spun and the van jolted forward.

"I wanna see it," she pleaded, hardly able to force the words past her parched lips.

"Just a minute, Klaya." Seth stroked her hair.

The van halted. Drew opened the door.

"Here we go," the woman called out.

Klaya propped her heavy head up in time to catch the fantastic blast. Spectacular flames and clouds of smoke rolled up into the sky. More cracks and explosions rocked the vehicle.

"Go," Drew yelled.

Her vision blurred, her breathing slowed, and the last thing she was able to fix her sight on, was a shadow that filled the back door, and her eyes slammed shut.

"We're losing her." The voices around her faded. "Klaya? Hang on, babe, please."

Chapter Sixteen

Klaya gasped and forced her eyes open. Panic shot through her; the scorch inside her upper body rippled through her veins.

"It's okay, sweetheart. It's over. You're safe now."

She dropped her throbbing head to the side to find Seth at her bedside. Her heart raced at the sight of him. "You're home now."

Shock rolled over her as his words sank in. She scanned the room for anything familiar. White cabinets with glass doors, medical supplies.... "Doc's office?"

"Yeah, we got you to Los Lobos; you had us pretty scared there. It was close, but he patched you up."

Klaya patted her chest and discovered thick layers of gauze wrapped around her. She spotted more cotton wrapped around her wrist.

"You spend far too much time in here. I'm beginning to wonder if you're crushing on Doc." Seth snickered.

"Our patient is up, I see." Bastian approached the bed, checked her eyes, and held her good wrist as he glanced at his watch. "I still can't get over how fast you heal." He shook his head with a grin.

"She's okay?" a voice called from the doorway.

"Drew?"

"Hey there." His smile warmed her heart. "Glad to see you're doing better."

"Why don't we give these two a minute, Doc?" Drew nudged Bastian's shoulder and the two men left the room.

"Seth?" Her chin quivered and her tears spilled down the sides of her face.

"Shhh, it's all right." He stood up and planted a tender kiss on her lips. "They're all gone. They won't hurt anyone ever again."

"They said they were scouting other groups of Cytaana out of the area. What if there are more of the hunters?"

"The threat here is gone. We'll let Drew and Ryker worry about any future problems. For now, it's

153

over."

Relief shifted to dread. "Rogue?" She shook her head. The vision of him going over the cliff sent a shock wave of grief through her.

"Hey, I wouldn't miss the party, babe," another voice rang out.

"Rogue?" Her throat grew thick. There, in the doorway, was the mass of blond curls and incredible green eyes she was convinced she'd never see again. "I thought you were...." She tried to catch her breath.

"Not a chance, we have too much to do together." He joined his brother at her side. "Listen, Doc warned us not to overwhelm you, so how about this?" Rogue leaned down and planted a feathery kiss on her lips. "You rest for a bit. We'll visit in a little while and bring you some food." He winked.

"And later we can stop by Gee's for a few tequila sunrises?" Seth smiled.

"With extra cherries." She giggled but winced when her chest muscles stung from the laughter.

**

It had been a long week, and she didn't recover as fast this time. Doc said they'd lost her twice, but he was able to save her. The bullet had missed her heart but nicked an artery. She was ordered on bed rest the entire week. The fresh scar on her wrist served as a constant reminder to look before she leaped, but it was also a badge of honor in her mind. This time, she took the fall so the ones she loved didn't have to. The brothers had lectured her relentlessly about her impulsive suicide mission; Griffith remained a cherished memory for her. She headed down to Gee's bar, as Drew had requested, and they planned to have a round in his honor.

The clouds rolled over and it began to sprinkle. A chill set in the air. Tonight, would be a great night to cuddle among her wolves. For now, she headed through the doors of the bar to catch up with her new family.

The place was empty, Klaya was surprised she was the first to arrive. She wandered over to the bar and plopped herself onto a stool.

Kayden the bartender peeked out from the kitchen door. "Oh, hey, Klaya, want a drink?"

"I most certainly do." She smiled.

"Gee, hurry up," he called back into the kitchen. "She's here." Kayden rushed over to the bar and placed a tall slender glass in front of her. He measured the tequila, poured the juice and grenadine, and topped it with a cherry and a straw. "Here you go, sunshine."

Crashes and bangs resonated from the kitchen. The muffled sound of Gee's voice made her chuckle. After a few more bangs and smashes, he let out a series of curse words. "Kayden?"

"I'm on it, boss." He rushed through the doors, and Gee came out.

"Get over here," he demanded. Klaya raced over into the warmth of his sensational bear hug.

She gasped at his strength. "Not so tight, big guy," she huffed with winded laughter.

"If you think I'm letting you go again, you're wrong." He kissed her cheek and set her down.

"Where is everyone?"

"I needed a little extra help." He winked and waved to the kitchen. "Follow me, my dear. I have a table for you."

Klaya grabbed her drink and traipsed behind the bear. At the far side of the room was a long table with several place settings. "What is this?" Happiness flooded her.

"Your welcome home feast." Rogue came out carrying a platter of sliced meat. He inched past her as she took a long whiff. Her mouth watered with the delectable smell.

"Venison," she cooed.

"And all the trimmings." Seth slipped past her with a bowl of potatoes.

Next Z snuck by with carrots then Allana with buns and gravy.

Klaya's heart warmed at the sight. "Thank you all...this is beautiful."

Rogue held out a chair for her then took his place beside her and Seth sat on her other side. Everyone else took their seats. Betty sat at her mate, Drew's side. Even Ripley joined along with Z, and Allana beside Bastian.

Kayden joined them with a tray of filled wine glasses. He handed everyone a drink, placed the tray down, and took his seat, too.

"It's been one hell of a month." Drew raised his glass and everyone did the same. "We lost a beloved comrade but gained a new member." He glanced to Klaya.

She bit her lips together to fight off the whimper threatening from deep inside.

"New friendships are forged and we avenged many. The pack is safe and Klaya is home now.

Here's to family." He toasted with Klaya. Glasses all around clinked and people sipped. Thea heartfelt toast that left her a little shattered inside. She missed her brother, Griffith, but she was thankful to be among the wolves.

After a full meal and a number of rounds, the pack parted ways and Klaya walked down the street, holding hands with the brothers.

"You okay, babe?" Rogue kissed the inside of her wrist.

"More than okay." She smiled.

"You've been so quiet." Seth massaged her palm with his thumb.

"I have, but I'm happy."

"You must be worn out?" Rogue grinned. "That's our place down at the far end."

Klaya eyed the quaint little bungalow down the way. "It's cute." She frowned.

"What's wrong?" Seth stopped and turned to face her.

"I miss our cave." She shrugged.

"We can visit there anytime." Rogue tucked a stray tendril of hair behind her ear.

"I'd like to."

Seth cupped her cheek. "There's something else. You seem a little sad."

"No. It's just...." Her bottom lip quivered.

"You can tell us?" Seth prompted.

"Back at the cellar...." She shuddered at the mere thought of the dungeon and her time there. "The sadistic pig told me, I'm not the last one."

"Cougar?" Rogue cocked his head. "There is the Goldspark clan of Shady Hearts?"

"I wondered if he meant the Cytaana." She frowned. "He said there was a handful he knew of, but I was the last one in this area."

"Do you want to search for them, babe?" Rogue squeezed her hand.

"Maybe, someday."

"You okay?" Seth gazed at her with adoring eyes.

She inhaled a sharp breath. "I am, I guess. I'm relieved I'm not the last Cytaana."

"Anytime you decide you want to, we'll go with you." Seth smiled.

"Thank you, both of you, for everything."

"We should tuck you in." Rogue grinned. "No funny business. Doc said you need your rest."

"I need something else first." She winked.

"Does it start with cherry stems?" Rogue licked his lips.

"Maybe...." she taunted.

Blondie picked her up. Klaya wrapped her arms around his neck and tucked her legs around his waist. Rogue devoured her lips with a long, intoxicating kiss.

"Don't be greedy, bro." Seth brushed her hair to the side and kissed her shoulder.

Klaya twisted sideways and gazed at her brown-eyed wolf with a grin. "I've got lots of catching up to do with you both." She cupped his face and drew him near for a taste of his sweet lips.

"We'd better take this inside before Drew kicks our asses." Rogue chuckled and set her on her feet. The three of them held hands and bolted toward the house.

About the Author

Born and raised in Toronto, Kali now resides in the exquisite eastern Ontario countryside where she enjoys the serenity of nature. When she isn't busy being the married mother of two, certified trainer or counselor extraordinaire, she shadows worlds of paranormal passion & intrigue.

Kali strives to create emotional, compelling stories and characters you can't help but love, hate and cheer for. Captivated by her love of dragons, gargoyles and everything paranormal, she pens these delightful creatures into epic tales of romance and adventure and often infuses her passions of martial arts, music and ironic twists even she didn't foresee.

A good cup of tea with the crackling fire gets her creative juices flowing in the wee hours of the night, when the house is quiet and she can type away to her heart's desire. Learn more at: www.kaliwillows.com

Also by Kali Willows